James Patrick

Winner of the
Hugo Award
Nebula Award
Locus Award
Asimov's Readers Poll
Nominated for the
Tiptree Award
Sturgeon Award
Seuin Award (Japan)

"He changes our attitudes and our perceptions and even
our understanding of what the short story can be, and he
does it in stories which are disturbing, clever, affecting,
funny, and unique in every sense of the word."
—Connie Willis

"James Patrick Kelly has written some of my very favorite
short stories. As a matter of fact, I get anxious when I haven't
read a Kelly story in a while. Can't we just clone him?"
—Kelly Link

"Against all law and likelihood, [he goes on] reinventing
himself each time out, always questioning the basic
premise of what a science fiction story can be, or a James
Patrick Kelly story, or a story in the first place."
—Jonathan Lethem

"What I guess I'm saying is that I like the way Jim Kelly writes
science fiction and makes it art. Jim entertains me and makes
me think and makes me feel—all without showing off."
—John Kessel

"He never behaves as a gaseous interstellar intellectual, yet he is nevertheless keenly and even somewhat scarily intelligent. Thinking back over the Kelly oeuvre, I'm struck not only by its solid craft but by its visionary qualities."
—Bruce Sterling

The First Law of Thermodynamics

plus

PM PRESS OUTSPOKEN AUTHORS SERIES

PM PRESS OUTSPOKEN AUTHORS SERIES

The First Law of Thermodynamics

plus

Someone Else's Problem

plus

Who Owns Cyberpunk?

and much more

James Patrick Kelly

PM PRESS | 2021

"Someone Else's Problem" is original to this volume.

"Itsy Bitsy Spider" first appeared in *Asimov's Science Fiction*, June 1997.

"The First Law of Thermodynamics" first appeared in *Intersections*, edited by John Kessel, Tor Books, January 1996.

"Donut Hole" is original to this volume.

"Who Owns Cyberpunk?" first appeared in *Strange Divisions and Alien Territories*, edited by Keith Brooke, Palgrave Macmillan, 2012.

"The Best Christmas Ever" first appeared in *SciFiction*, May 2004.

The First Law of Thermodynamics
James Patrick Kelly © 2021
This edition © PM Press

ISBN (paperback): 978-1-62963-885-0
ISBN (ebook): 978-1-62963-904-8
LCCN: 2020947226

Series editor: Terry Bisson
Cover design by John Yates/www.stealworks.com
Author photograph by Pamela Kelly
Insides by Jonathan Rowland

10 9 8 7 6 5 4 3 2 1

Printed in the USA

CONTENTS

Someone Else's Problem

Cast: CASSIE, a human woman
            FRANCIS, a human man, her husband
            TWEEL, an alien in human form

Time: the present
Setting: A suburban living room

At rise: CASSIE and FRANCIS are absorbed in the Sunday newspaper.
They are not paying particularly close attention to one another.

CASSIE: CRISPR.
FRANCIS: Say again?
CASSIE: CRISPR, *CRISPR*! Clustered regularly interspaced short palindromic repeats.
FRANCIS: Umm . . . translation, please?
She doesn't answer, and he gives her an annoyed stare.
Cass? Mind trying again in English?
CASSIE: (*absently*) It can cut DNA. Edit your genome.
FRANCIS: Have you got the Arts section? I'll trade you for Travel.
They exchange sections. Both read for a few beats.
FRANCIS: Hey, do you want to see *Captain Marvel*? Missed it in the theaters but that new Disney Channel I signed up for has it.

CASSIE: Do we really have to watch another of your superhero movies?

FRANCIS: This one is a girl. (*catches himself*) A woman. She's Brie Larson.

CASSIE: The one from Room?

FRANCIS: Huh, forgot she was in that. All that arty claustrophobia creeped me out. No, I was thinking of her in the Kong movie. *Skull Island*. So? Supposed to be good. *Captain Marvel*.

CASSIE: (*absently*) Okay.

FRANCIS: Okay yes? Or okay you're acknowledging my existence? (*beat*) Cassie!

CASSIE: We could be superheroes, you know.

FRANCIS is confused.

CASSIE: With CRISPR. (*impatiently*) I'm reading about CRISPR.

FRANCIS: Superheroes. Sounds like a lot of work. Not for the likes of us.

CASSIE: Says here some guy in China made a couple of super-smart twins. Used CRISPR to mess with their genes.

FRANCIS: Takeaway for dinner and movie night. Thai? Indian?

CASSIE: We could be super-smart. Or maybe super-strong.

FRANCIS: Super-invisible?

CASSIE: I don't think there's a gene for that. What's to stop them from creating a whole new species of super-people? You know, like to replace us?

FRANCIS: Nothing we can do about that. (*opens his cell phone*) There's that new place, Shalimar Something.

CASSIE: Tweel is late. (*looks out the window*) She's an alien. They're never late.

FRANCIS: She was late two times ago.

CASSIE: Where did you put the Travel section? (*finds it, reads*) Oh, no. Vail is closing.

FRANCIS: I read that. Okay, *Captain Marvel* got 78 percent on Rotten Tomatoes. Hello? 78 percent?

CASSIE: I mean, where are we going to ski in the Rockies now?

FRANCIS: They say Canada still gets snow. Whistler? Banff?

CASSIE: But I love Colorado.

FRANCIS: That's global warming for you. Good thing we didn't buy that condo you wanted.

CASSIE: I feel sorry for the Fullers.

FRANCIS: The Fullers?

CASSIE: They owned that B&B where we stayed that time.

FRANCIS: Oh, you mean Alice and what's-his-name. Wait, their last name was Fuller?

CASSIE: His name was Harlan. Of course you remember her and not him.

FRANCIS: Well, he didn't make those great blueberry scones.

CASSIE: Scones. (*sarcastically*) Oh, is *that* what you were always staring at?

FRANCIS: (*changing the subject*) You're right, they probably are screwed. It's too bad. Whatever is that town going to do without skiing?

CASSIE: Or all the spruces. The poor blue spruces.

FRANCIS: What's wrong with the spruces again?

CASSIE: Pine beetles. Some invader bug that drinks all the sap. Moved north with the warm winters. Remember how Harlan was showing us the white scale on the needles?

FRANCIS: I thought those were pine trees.

CASSIE: Blue spruce. I'm pretty sure.

FRANCIS: They'll figure it out. Not our problem.

CASSIE: (*looks out window*) There she is. (*beat*) Oh my god, she must have been next door with the Navarros. No way they're her kind of people.

FRANCIS: You think they were giving her a hard time? Jose can be pretty stubborn.

CASSIE: But Gail Navarro is the one with the big mouth. Like when she tried to get us to sign that petition about the bees and pesticides.

FRANCIS: Troublemakers, both of them.

CASSIE: And the way their kids are always shrieking. Tweel wouldn't stand still for that.

FRANCIS: No alien would!

CASSIE: (*still looking out the window*) She's coming up the driveway. Get the door before she knocks, would you, Francis? Show her that at least we know what's what.

FRANCIS: On it!

He exits. CASSIE straightens up the newspaper, then stands beside her chair, waiting. FRANCIS and TWEEL enter together. FRANCIS is walking backward, TWEEL walking forward. Her hand rests on his forehead. She backs him to his chair and gives a push. He sits. TWEEL turns to CASSIE, places her hand on her forehead, pushes. CASSIE sits. They smile and nod at each other for reassurance.

CASSIE: You're looking well, Tweel. Isn't she, Francis?

FRANCIS: Very human. I'd be fooled. Anyone would.

TWEEL ignores them, sorts through the paper, scanning headlines, then dropping sections on the floor. She continues while they try to make conversation.

CASSIE: You're doing something different with your hair. I like it. Makes you look . . .

FRANCIS: (*interrupts*) . . . distinguished.

CASSIE: . . . younger.

FRANCIS: Young but distinguished. And perceptive. Can we get you something? What have we got, Cass?

CASSIE: Coke, Coke Zero, Cherry Coke Zero, for sure. Tea and coffee. Stoned Wheat Thins. (*to FRANCIS*) Is there any of that dill Havarti left?

FRANCIS: I'll check.

He starts to get up but TWEEL stares him back down. TWEEL discards the last of the newspaper, takes the translator out of her pocket, holds it in front of CASSIE and turns it on. TWEEL utters one short inarticulate questioning bark in her language. CASSIE understands this.

CASSIE: Why? Is there something wrong with reading the paper?

FRANCIS: We like to stay informed.

TWEEL aims the translator at FRANCIS and gives two questioning barks, which FRANCIS understands.

FRANCIS: Because . . . umm . . . I don't know. So we can see what's coming. Maybe take action. (*looks to CASSIE for support*) But *appropriate* action.

TWEEL gives an unhappy bark.

CASSIE: Or not!

TWEEL brings the translator very close to CASSIE, who tries to back away. TWEEL barks twice.

CASSIE: Sorry, I didn't understand that one. You want me to be more what? More peaceful?

TWEEL gives one negative bark.

CASSIE: Satisfied?

FRANCIS: Oh, Cassie's satisfied. We both live very satisfied lives.

TWEEL gives another negative bark.

CASSIE: Complacent! (*understanding*) She wants me . . . us . . . to be more complacent.

FRANCIS: Oh sure. We can do that. Easy enough—we're halfway there already.

TWEEL crumples some newspaper, drops it on CASSIE's lap and barks twice.

CASSIE: (*as if repeating what TWEEL said*) There's nothing *we* can do about it. Right.

TWEEL aims the translator at FRANCIS and barks.

FRANCIS: (*as if repeating what TWEEL said*) Because *they'll* figure it out. (*confused*) Who'll figure what out?

TWEEL gives a bark.

CASSIE: Someone. Someone who isn't us will figure whatever needs figuring out . . . out.

FRANCIS: Got it. (*nods uncertainly*) Makes sense.

TWEEL turns the translator off, pockets it and exits, paying no attention to them as they say goodbye.

CASSIE: Thank you!

FRANCIS: See you next time!

They sit for a moment looking at each other.

FRANCIS: Did we do okay?

CASSIE: I don't know. I hope so.

FRANCIS: Do you think it's okay to stand up?

CASSIE: Maybe give it a minute.

FRANCIS: Okay. (*pats himself as if checking to see if he's all there*) That was the most intense one yet.

CASSIE: I want one of those sparkly things. It looks like something from your Doctor Who.

FRANCIS: It isn't my Doctor Who. It's everybody's. Did she have to make such a mess?

   (*He leans over and start picking up newspaper*)

I mean really, where are the manners?

CASSIE: She's from space.

FRANCIS: (*now kneels on the floor, cleaning up*) Complacency, who would've thought?

CASSIE: I'm not even sure what that means.

FRANCIS: Not giving a shit.

CASSIE: I guess. (*leans to peer out the window*) I think Tweel is gone to wherever they go . . . *Oh my God!*

FRANCIS: What? Cassie? What is it?

CASSIE: Francis, you've got to see this. (*points*) The Navarros' house. It's gone.

FRANCIS: Gone? Gone where?

He scrambles next to her, stares out the window, gasps.

CASSIE: Nothing but a hole. And dirt.

FRANCIS: How is that even possible? I mean, look, their lawn is still perfect. Not a leaf off the rhododendrons.

CASSIE: And the swing set . . .

They look at each other in horror.

FRANCIS: It's Sunday. They were probably at church. Look, here come the cops. It's their problem.

They slide back into their chairs.

FRANCIS: We didn't see anything. We were reading the paper.

CASSIE: But Francis . . .

He puts his arms around her.

FRANCIS: Not our problem, Cass. They'll have to figure it out. Someone. Not us.

CASSIE: There's nothing we can do?

FRANCIS: No. (*beat*) Not anymore.

blackout

Itsy Bitsy Spider

WHEN I FOUND OUT that my father was still alive after all these years and living at Strawberry Fields, I thought he'd gotten just what he deserved. Retroburbs are where the old, scared people go to hide. I'd always pictured the people in them as deranged losers. Visiting some fantasy world like the Disneys or Carlucci's Carthage is one thing, moving to one is another. Sure, 2038 is messy, but it's a hell of a lot better than nineteen-sixty-whatever.

Now that I'd arrived at 144 Bluejay Way, I realized the place was worse than I had imagined. Strawberry Fields was pretending to be some long, lost suburb of the late twentieth century, except that it had the sterile monotony of cheap VR. It was clean, all right, and neat, but it was everywhere the same. And the scale was wrong. The lots were squeezed together and all the houses had shrunk—like the dreams of their owners. They were about the size of a one car garage, modular units tarted up at the factory to look like ranches, with old double-hung storm windows and hardened siding of harvest gold, barn red, forest green. Of course, there were no real garages; faux Mustangs and VW buses cruised the quiet streets. Their carbrains were listening for a summons from Barbara Chesley next door at 142, or the Goltzes across the street, who might be headed to Penny Lanes to bowl a few frames, or the hospital to die.

There was a beach chair with blue nylon webbing on the front stoop of 144 Bluejay Way. A brick walk led to it, dividing two patches

of carpet moss, green as a dream. There were names and addresses printed in huge lightstick letters on all the doors in the neighborhood; no
doubt many Strawberry Fielders were easily confused. The owner of this
one was Peter Fancy. He had been born Peter Fanelli but had legally
taken his stage name not long after his first success as Prince Hal in
Henry IV Part I. I was a Fancy too; the name was one of the few things
of my father's I had kept.

I stopped at the door and let it look me over. "You're Jen," it said.

"Yes." I waited in vain for it to open or to say something else. "I'd
like to see Mr. Fancy, please." The old man's house had worse manners
than he did. "He knows I'm coming," I said. "I sent him several mes-
sages." Which he had never answered, but I didn't mention that.

"Just a minute," said the door. "She'll be right with you."

She? The idea that he might be with another woman now hadn't
occurred to me. I'd lost track of my father a long time ago—on purpose. The last time we'd actually visited overnight was when I was
twenty. Mom gave me a ticket to Port Gemini where he was doing the
Shakespeare in Space program. The orbital was great, but staying with
him was like being underwater. I think I must have held my breath for
the entire week. After that there were a few, sporadic calls, a couple
of awkward dinners—all at his instigation. Then twenty-three years of
nothing.

I never hated him, exactly. When he left, I just decided to show sol-
idarity with Mom and be done with him. If acting was more important
than his family, then to hell with Peter Fancy. Mom was horrified when
I told her how I felt. She cried and claimed the divorce was as much her
fault as his. It was too much for me to handle; I was only eleven years
old when they separated. I needed to be on *someone's* side and so I had
chosen her. She never did stop trying to talk me into finding him again,

even though after a while it only made me mad at her. For the past few years, she'd been warning me that I'd developed a warped view of men.

But she was a smart woman, my mom—a winner. Sure, she'd had troubles, but she'd founded three companies, was a millionaire by twenty-five. I missed her.

A lock clicked and the door opened. Standing in the dim interior was a little girl in a gold and white checked dress. Her dark, curly hair was tied in a ribbon. She was wearing white ankle socks and black Mary Jane shoes that were so shiny they had to be plastic. There was a Band-Aid on her left knee.

"Hello, Jen. I was hoping you'd really come." Her voice surprised me. It was resonant, impossibly mature. At first glance I'd guessed she was three, maybe four; I'm not much good at guessing kids' ages. Now I realized that this must be a bot—a made person.

"You look just like I thought you would." She smiled, stood on tiptoe and raised a delicate little hand over her head. I had to bend to shake it. The hand was warm, slightly moist and very realistic. She had to belong to Strawberry Fields; there was no way my father could afford a bot with skin this real.

"Please come in." She waved on the lights. "We're so happy you're here." The door closed behind me.

The playroom took up almost half of the little house. Against one wall was a miniature kitchen. Toy dishes were drying in a rack next to the sink; the pink refrigerator barely came up to my waist. The table was full-sized; it had two normal chairs and a booster chair. Opposite this was a bed with a ruffled Pumpkin Patty bedspread. About a dozen dolls and stuffed animals were arranged along the far edge of the mattress. I recognized most of them: Pooh, Mr. Moon, Baby Rollypolly, the Sleepums, Big Bird. And the wallpaper was familiar too: Oz figures like

Toto and the Wizard and the Cowardly Lion on a field of Munchkin blue.

"We had to make a few changes," said the bot. "Do you like it?"

The room seemed to tilt then. I took a small, unsteady step and everything righted itself. My dolls, my wallpaper, the chest of drawers from Grandma Fanelli's cottage in Hyannis. I stared at the bot and recognized her for the first time.

She was me.

"What is this," I said, "some kind of sick joke?" I felt like I'd just been slapped in the face.

"Is something wrong?" the bot said. "Tell me. Maybe we can fix it."

I swiped at her and she danced out of reach. I don't know what I would have done if I had caught her. Maybe smashed her through the picture window onto the patch of front lawn or shaken her until pieces started falling off. But the bot wasn't responsible, my father was. Mom would never have defended him if she'd known about *this*. The old bastard. I couldn't believe it. Here I was, shuddering with anger, after years of feeling nothing for him.

There was an interior door just beyond some shelves filled with old-fashioned paper books. I didn't take time to look as I went past, but I knew that Dr. Seuss and A.A. Milne and L. Frank Baum would be on those shelves. The door had no knob.

"Open up," I shouted. It ignored me, so I kicked it. "Hey!"

"Jennifer." The bot tugged at the back of my jacket. "I must ask you . . ."

"You can't have me!" I pressed my ear to the door. Silence. "I'm not this thing you made." I kicked it again. "You hear?"

Suddenly an announcer was shouting in the next room. ". . . *into the post to Russell, who kicks it out to Havlichek all alone at the top of the key, he shoots . . . and Baylor with the strong rebound."* The asshole was trying to drown me out.

"If you don't come away from that door right now," said the bot, "I'm calling security."

"What are they going to do?" I said. "I'm the long-lost daughter, here for a visit. And who the hell are you, anyway?"

"I'm bonded to him, Jen. Your father is no longer competent to handle his own affairs. I'm his legal guardian."

"Shit." I kicked the door one last time, but my heart wasn't in it. I shouldn't have been surprised that he had slipped over the edge. He was almost ninety.

"If you want to sit and talk, I'd like that very much." The bot gestured toward a banana yellow beanbag chair. "Otherwise, I'm going to have to ask you to leave."

# #

It was the shock of seeing the bot, I told myself—I'd reacted like a hurt little girl. But I was grown woman and it was time to start behaving like one. I wasn't here to let Peter Fancy worm his way back into my feelings. I had come because of Mom.

"Actually," I said, "I'm here on business." I opened my purse. "If you're running his life now, I guess this is for you." I passed her the envelope and settled back, tucking my legs beneath me. There is no way for an adult to sit gracefully in a beanbag chair.

She slipped the check out. "It's from Mother." She paused, then corrected herself, "Her estate." She didn't seem surprised.

"Yes."

"It's too generous."

"That's what I thought."

"She must've taken care of you too?"

"I'm fine." I wasn't about to discuss the terms of Mom's will with my father's toy daughter.

"I would've like to have known her," said the bot. She slid the check back into the envelope and set it aside. "I've spent a lot of time imagining Mother."

I had to work hard not to snap at her. Sure, this bot had at least a human equivalent intelligence and would be a free citizen someday, assuming she didn't break down first. But she had a cognizor for a brain and a heart fabricated in a vat. How could she possibly imagine my mom, especially when all she had to go on was whatever lies *he* had told her?

"So how bad is he?"

She gave me a sad smile and shook her head. "Some days are better than others. He has no clue who President Huong is or about the quake but he can still recite the dagger scene from *Macbeth*. I haven't told him that Mother died. He'd just forget it ten minutes later."

"Does he know what you are?"

"I am many things, Jen."

"Including me."

"You're a role I'm playing, not who I am." She stood. "Would you like some tea?"

"Okay." I still wanted to know why Mom had left my father $438,000 in her will. If he couldn't tell me, maybe the bot could.

She went to her kitchen, opened a cupboard and took out a regular-sized cup. It looked like a bucket in her little hand. "I don't suppose you still drink Constant Comment?"

His favorite. I had long since switched to rafallo. "That's fine." I remembered when I was a kid my father used to brew cups for the two of us from the same bag because Constant Comment was so expensive. "I thought they went out of business long ago."

"I mix my own. I'd be interested to hear how accurate you think the recipe is."

"I suppose you know how I like it?"

She chuckled.

"So does he need the money?"

The microwave dinged. "Very few actors get rich," said the bot. I didn't think there had been microwaves in the sixties, but then strict historical accuracy wasn't really the point of Strawberry Fields. "Especially when they have a weakness for Shakespeare."

"Then how come he lives here and not in some flop? And how did he afford you?"

She pinched sugar between her index finger and thumb, then rubbed them together over the cup. It was something I still did, but only when I was by myself. A nasty habit; Mom used to yell at him for teaching it to me. "I was a gift." She shook a teabag loose from a canister shaped like an acorn and plunged it into the boiling water. "From Mother."

The bot offered the cup to me; I accepted it nervelessly. "That's not true." I could feel the blood draining from my face.

"I can lie if you'd prefer, but I'd rather not." She pulled the booster chair away from the table and turned it to face me. "There are many things about themselves that they never told us, Jen. I've always wondered why that was."

I felt logy and a little stupid, as if I had just woken from a thirty-year nap. "She just gave you to him?"

"And bought him this house, paid all his bills, yes."

"But why?"

"*You* knew her," said the bot. "I was hoping you could tell me."

I couldn't think of what to say or do. Since there was a cup in my hand, I took a sip. For an instant the scent of tea and dried oranges carried me back to when I was a little girl and was sitting in Grandma Fanelli's kitchen in a wet bathing suit, drinking Constant Comment that my father had made to keep my teeth from chattering. There were knots like brown eyes in the pine walls, and the green linoleum was slick where I had dripped on it.

"Well?"

"It's good," I said absently and raised the cup to her. "No really, just like I remember."

She clapped her hands in excitement. "So," said the bot. "What was Mother like?"

It was an impossible question, so I tried to let it bounce off me. But then neither of us said anything; we just stared at each other across a yawning gulf of time and experience. In the silence, the question stuck. Mom had died three months ago, and this was the first time since the funeral that I'd thought of her as she really had been—not the papery ghost in the hospital room. I remembered how, after the divorce, she always took my calls when she was at the office, even if it was late, and how she used to step on imaginary brakes whenever I drove her anywhere and how grateful I was that she didn't cry when I told her that Rob and I were getting divorced. I thought about Easter eggs and raspberry Pop Tarts and when she sent me to Antibes for a year when I was fourteen and that perfume she wore on my father's opening nights and the way they used to waltz on the patio at the house in Waltham.

"*West is walking the ball up court, setting his offense with fifteen seconds to go on the shot clock, nineteen in the half . . .*"

The beanbag chair that I was in faced the picture window. Behind me, I could hear the door next to the bookcase open.

"Jones and Goodrich are in each other's jerseys down low and now Chamberlin swings over and calls for the ball on the weak side . . ."

I twisted around to look over my shoulder. The great Peter Fancy was making his entrance.

#

Mom once told me that when she met my father, he was typecast playing men that women fall hopelessly in love with. He'd had great successes as Stanley Kowalski in *Streetcar* and Sky Masterson in *Guys and Dolls* and the Vicomte de Valmont in *Les Liaisons Dangereuses*. The years had eroded his good looks but had not obliterated them; from a distance he was still a handsome man. He had a shock of close-cropped white hair. The beautiful cheekbones were still there; the chin was as sharply defined as it had been in his first headshot. His gray eyes were distant and a little dreamy, as if he were preoccupied with the War of the Roses or the problem of evil.

"Jen," he said, "what's going on out here?" He still had the big voice that could reach into the second balcony without a mike. I thought for a moment he was talking to me.

"We have company, Daddy," said the bot, in a four-year-old trill that took me by surprise. "A lady."

"I can see that it's a lady, sweetheart." He took a hand from the pocket of his jeans, stroked the touchpad on his belt and his exolegs walked him stiffly across the room. "I'm Peter Fancy," he said.

"The lady is from Strawberry Fields." The bot swung around behind my father. She shot me a look that made the terms and conditions of my continued presence clear: if I broke the illusion, I was out. "She came by to see if everything is all right with our house." The bot disturbed me even more, now that she sounded like young Jen Fancy.

As I heaved myself out the beanbag chair, my father gave me one of those lopsided, flirting grins I knew so well. "Does the lady have a name?" He must have shaved just for the company, because now that he had come close I could see that he had a couple of fresh nicks. There was a button-sized patch of gray whiskers by his ear that he had missed altogether.

"Her name is Ms. Johnson," said the bot. It was my ex, Rob's, last name. I had never been Jennifer Johnson.

"Well, Ms. Johnson," he said, hooking thumbs in his pants pockets. "The water in my toilet is brown."

"I'll . . . um . . . see that it's taken care of." I was at a loss for what to say next, then inspiration struck. "Actually, I had another reason for coming." I could see the bot stiffen. "I don't know if you've seen *Yesterday*, our little newsletter? Anyway, I was talking to Mrs. Chesley next door and she told me that you were an actor once. I was wondering if I might interview you. Just a few questions, if you have the time. I think your neighbors might . . ."

"Were?" he said, drawing himself up. "*Once*? Madame, I am now an actor and will always be."

"My Daddy's famous," said the bot.

I cringed at that; it was something I used to say. My father squinted at me. "What did you say your name was?"

"Johnson," I said. "Jane Johnson."

"And you're a reporter? You're sure you're not a critic?"

"Positive."

He seemed satisfied. "I'm Peter Fancy." He extended his right hand to shake. The hand was spotted and bony and it trembled like a reflection in a lake. Clearly whatever magic—or surgeon's skill—it was that had preserved my father's face had not extended to his extremities. I was so disturbed by his infirmity that I took his cold hand in mine and pumped it three, four times. It was dry as a page of one of the bot's dead books. When I let go, the hand seemed steadier. He gestured at the beanbag.

"Sit," he said. "Please."

After I had settled in, he tapped the touchpad and stumped over to the picture window. "Barbara Chesley is a broken and bitter old woman," he said, "and I will not have dinner with her under any circumstances, do you understand?" He peered up Bluejay Way and down.

"Yes, Daddy," said the bot.

"I believe she voted for Nixon, so she has no reason to complain now." Apparently satisfied that the neighbor weren't sneaking up on us, he leaned against the windowsill, facing me. "Mrs. Thompson, I think today may well be a happy one for both of us. I have an announcement." He paused for effect. "I've been thinking of Lear again."

The bot settled onto one of her little chairs. "Oh, Daddy, that's wonderful."

"It's the only one of the big four I haven't done," said my father. "I was set for a production in Stratford, Ontario, back in '99; Polly Matthews was to play Cordelia. Now there was an actor; she could bring tears to a stone. But then my wife Hannah had one of her bad times and I had to withdraw so I could take care of Jen. The two of us stayed down at my mother's cottage on the Cape; I wasted the entire season tending bar. And when Hannah came out of rehab, she decided that she didn't want to be married to an underemployed actor anymore, so things were tight for a while. She had all the money, so I had to scramble—spent almost two years on the road. But I think it might have been for the best. I was only forty-eight. Too old for Hamlet, too young for Lear. My Hamlet was very well received, you know. There were overtures from PBS about a taping, but that was when the BBC decided to do the Shakespeare series with that doctor, what was his name? Jonathan Miller. So instead of Peter Fancy, we had Derek Jacobi, whose brilliant idea it was to roll across the stage, frothing his lines like a rabid raccoon. You'd think he'd seen an alien, not his father's ghost. Well, that was another missed opportunity, except, of course, that I was too young. Ripeness is all, eh? So I still have Lear to do. Unfinished business. My comeback."

He bowed, then pivoted solemnly so that I saw him in profile, framed by the picture window. "Where have I been? Where am I? Fair daylight?" He held up a trembling hand and blinked at it uncomprehendingly. "I know not what to say. I swear these are not my hands."

Suddenly the bot was at his feet. "O look upon me, sir," she said, in her childish voice, "and hold your hand in benediction o'er me."

"Pray, do not mock me." My father gathered himself in the flood of morning light. "I am a very foolish, fond old man, fourscore and upward, not an hour more or less; and to deal plainly, I fear I am not in my perfect mind."

He stole a look in my direction, as if to gauge my reaction to his impromptu performance. A frown might have stopped him, a word would have crushed him. Maybe I should have but I was afraid he'd start talking about Mom again, telling me things I didn't want to know. So I watched instead, transfixed.

"Methinks I should know you..." He rested his hand briefly on the bot's head. "... and know this stranger." He fumbled at the controls and the exolegs carried him across the room toward me. As he drew nearer, he seemed to sluff off the years. "Yet I am mainly ignorant what place this is; and all the skill I have remembers not these garments, nor I know not where I did lodge last night." It was Peter Fancy who stopped before me; his face a mere kiss away from mine. "Do not laugh at me; for, as I am a man, I think this lady to be my child. Cordelia."

He was staring right at me, into me, knifing through make-believe indifference to the wound I'd nursed all these years, the one that had never healed. He seemed to expect a reply, only I didn't have the line. A tiny, sad squeaky voice within me was whimpering, *You left me and you got exactly what you deserve.* But my throat tightened and choked it off.

The bot cried, "And so I am! I am!"

But she had distracted him. I could see confusion begin to deflate him. "Be your tears wet? Yes, faith. I pray . . . weep not. If you have poison for me, I will drink it. I know you do not love me . . ."

He stopped and his brow wrinkled. "It's something about the sisters," he muttered.

"Yes," said the bot, "'. . . for your sisters have done me wrong . . .'"

"Don't feed me the fucking lines!" he shouted at her. "I'm Peter Fancy, goddamn it!"

#

After she calmed him down, we had lunch. She let him make the peanut butter and banana sandwiches while she heated up some Campbell's tomato and rice soup, which she poured from a can made of actual metal. The sandwiches were lumpy because he had hacked the bananas into chunks the size of walnuts. She tried to get him to tell me about the daylilies blooming in the backyard and the old Boston Garden and the time he and Mom had had breakfast with Bobby Kennedy. She asked whether he wanted TV dinner or pot pie for dinner. He refused all her conversational gambits. He only ate half a bowl of soup.

He pushed back from the table and announced that it was her nap time. The bot put up a perfunctory fuss, although it was clear that it was my father who was tired out. However, the act seemed to perk him up. Another role for his resume: the doting father. "I'll tell you what," he said. "We'll play your game, sweetheart. But just once—otherwise you'll be cranky tonight."

The two of them perched on the edge of the bot's bed next to Big Bird and the Sleepums. My father started to sing and the bot immediately joined in.

"The itsy bitsy spider went up the waterspout."

Their gestures were almost mirror images, except that his ruined hands actually looked like spiders as they climbed into the air.

"Down came the rain and washed the spider out."

The bot beamed at him as if he were the only person in the world.

"Out came the sun and dried up all the rain.

"And the itsy bitsy spider went up the spout again."

When his arms were once again raised over his head, she giggled and hugged him. He let them fall around her, returning her embrace. "That's a good girl," he said. "That's my Jenny."

The look on his face told me that I had been wrong: this was no act. It was as real to him as it was to me. I had tried hard not to, but I still remembered how the two of us always used to play together, Daddy and Jenny, Jen and Dad.

Waiting for Mommy to come home.

He kissed her and she snuggled under the blankets. I felt my eyes stinging.

"But if you do the play," she said, "when will you be back?"

"What play?"

"That one you were telling me. The king and his daughters."

"There's no such play, Jenny." He sifted her black curls through hands. "I'll never leave you, don't worry now. Never again." He rose unsteadily and caught himself on the chest of drawers.

"Nighty noodle," said the bot.

"Pleasant dreams, sweetheart," said my father. "I love you."

"I love you too."

I expected him to say something to me, but he didn't even seem to realize that I was still in the room. He shambled across the playroom, opened the door to his bedroom and went in.

"I'm sorry about that." said the bot, speaking again as an adult.

"Don't be," I said. I coughed—something in my throat. "It was fine. I was very . . . touched."

"He's usually a lot happier. Sometimes he works in the garden." The bot pulled the blankets aside and swung her legs out of the bed. "He likes to vacuum."

"Yes."

"I take good care of him."

I nodded and reached for my purse. "I can see that." I had to go. "Is it enough?"

She shrugged. "He's my daddy."

"I meant the money. Because if it's not, I'd like to help."

"Thank you. He'd appreciate that."

The front door opened for me, but I paused before stepping out into Strawberry Fields. "What about . . . after?"

"When he dies? My bond terminates. He said he'd leave the house to me. I know you could contest that, but I'll need to sell in order to pay for my twenty-year maintenance."

"No, no. That's fine. You deserve it."

She came to the door and looked up at me, little Jen Fancy and the woman she would never become.

"You know, it's you he loves," she said. "I'm just a stand-in."

"He loves his little girl," I said. "Doesn't do me any good—I'm forty-seven."

"It could if you let it." She frowned. "I wonder if that's why Mother did all this. So you'd find out."

"Or maybe she was just plain sorry." I shook my head. She was a smart woman, my mom. I would've liked to have known her.

"So Ms. Fancy, maybe you can visit us again sometime." The bot grinned and shook my hand. "Daddy's usually in a good mood after his nap. He sits out front on his beach chair and waits for the ice cream truck. He always buys us some. Our favorite is Yellow Submarine. It's vanilla with fat butterscotch swirls, dipped in white chocolate. I know it sounds kind of odd, but it's good."

"Yes," I said absently, thinking about all the things Mom had told me about my father. I was hearing them now for the first time. "That might be nice."

"Encounter with a Gadget Guy"

James Patrick Kelly interviewed by Terry Bisson

You are often seen hiking in the New England mountains. What's the most awesome thing you've encountered there?

The view from Mount Willard looking south down Crawford Notch on a clear early autumn day.

I was a Boy Scout and so picked up the hiking habit early. I continue to be active outdoors year-round because the endorphin high is my drug of choice these days. I jog between fifteen and twenty miles a week and try to compete in at least one 5K or 10K road race a year. In the summer I wake up and swim half a mile first thing. In the winter I usually reach for my snowshoes or cross-country skis. All this exercise is actually a career move; I do my best story doctoring when I'm out of breath.

If you could have a drink with a dead SF writer (not a friend), who would it be?

I'm tempted to say Paul Linebarger, aka the great Cordwainer Smith, but instead I'm going to sidestep this one just a bit. Raymond Chandler famously had no use whatsoever for science fiction. In a letter near the end of his life he wrote a vicious parody of a scene from an imagined SF story, and ended the note with this question: "They pay brisk money for this crap?"

But many science fiction writers have been influenced by Chandler, and I am one of them. In fact, I've read and reread all the novels and stories, most of the letters, and several of the biographies. I've paid homage to Chandler more than once in my fiction and intend to do it again.

In addition to being a bit of a snob, Chandler was also an alcoholic, so I realize that drinks might be a chore. After all, I *am* an SF writer and have been sober now for some twelve years. But hey, I'd be willing to fall off the wagon for an evening if it meant connecting with the man who had Philip Marlowe say, "I needed a drink. I needed a lot of life insurance. I needed a vacation. I needed a home in the country. What I had was a coat, a hat, and a gun."

How Irish are you?

Other than my brazenly Hibernian name, not very. The ancestral Irish immigrant arrived on these shores before the Civil War. On my mother's side, however, I'm second-generation Hungarian. My grandparents were born there and English was their second language.

But a kind of ersatz Irishness did impact my life. I attended the University of Notre Dame, of Fighting Irish football fame, in part because my dad followed their team. I think it was his oblique way of paying homage to our heritage. For the record, Notre Dame and I did not get along. Why did I choose an all-male school at the height of the sexual revolution? It's still a mystery to me! As soon as I realized my mistake, I loaded up on extra courses so I could graduate in three years. This was easier than it sounds; I was an English major.

Ever do hack work?

After escaping from Notre Dame, I started Real Life in the mail room of an architectural engineering company with offices throughout New England. As it turned out, what was most useful to this company was my ability to write comprehensible sentences. This skill, I discovered, was thin on the ground in AE firms. I began translating building proposals from engineering into English, and then writing press releases and promotional materials for the office I worked in, and then for the entire company. By the time I retired at the ripe old age of twenty-seven to write full time, I had the title of coordinator of public relations.

Early in my career I would have loved to write Star Trek novels, but I never found out what buttons to press to wrangle an invite.

You were at Clarion twice. Did you graduate or did they kick you out?
I flunked denouement. Thankfully, they let me make it up.

Back in the early days of Clarion, when it was still at Michigan State, attending more than once was rare but not unheard-of. But when I went the first time, it was drilled into us that the rule was *one and done.* For most students Clarion is an overwhelming experience. It certainly was for me. Not only did it vastly improve my command of the craft, but it validated my outrageous dream of becoming a writer. The magic of the workshop is that when smart people—your instructors and your fellow students—treat you like a writer, you convince yourself that they must be right!

And then the six weeks are over, and you return to your job and your real life. You have to work extra hard to catch up at work and on your relationships at home. Then the rejection slips land, and you doubt—what were you thinking?—and you find yourself deep in the dreaded post-Clarion depression. Happened to me, big time. I sold one silly story (that I have since struck from my bibliography) after Clarion and then there were months and months and deadening months of nothing. My career in public relations took off and consumed my fiction writing time. As I watched the dream fade, I wrote an impassioned letter to the late Glenn Wright, then Clarion director, begging him to break the rules and let me return to try to regain my momentum. That letter was probably the best writing I'd done since leaving East Lansing, and when Glenn passed it on to Damon Knight and Kate Wilhelm, they agreed.

They probably shouldn't have, although I doubt I would have had the same career, or maybe any career, if they had turned me down. One and done is a sound policy, although it is the case that several talented writers have attended the six-week Odyssey Writers' Workshop and then have gone to one of the Clarions. And Clarion grads have received degrees from the Stonecoast Creative Writing MFA program where I used to teach or gone from Stonecoast to Clarion. In any event, I did the workshop again. I realized later that one important outcome of going was that it killed my career at the architectural engineering company. They were willing to accommodate one six-week leave of absence, but a second one two years later was too much.

And the other outcome was that I finally passed denouement. As that second Clarion was coming to an end, I was pulling all-nighters to finish a story. I remember that it got critiqued on the second-to-last or maybe the last day. Damon and Kate, who founded Clarion and who always team taught the last two weeks, were writers in residence. The story was about an ambitious woman scientist who, against her better judgment, participated in an unspeakable experiment and in the process, all but wrecked her marriage. After much techno-mayhem, she alone was left of the research team; the experiment had succeeded at a horrific cost. In the denouement, she retreated in a daze to her office where she found a dozen roses from her estranged husband—a peace offering. In the version I workshopped, she decided impulsively to take the bouquet, go to him, and leave everything else behind. It was a bland conclusion to a There-Are-Some-Things-We-Are-Not-Meant-To-Know story. In her critique, Kate story-doctored my ending. She suggested that I have my hero toss all but a single flower out, stick that one in a bud vase, and sit down to write up the experiment, which would make her the new director of the lab. All it took was two sentences and one red rose to transform the piece into a chilling and powerful Scientist-Loses-Her-Soul story. This story—"Death Therapy"—was my second sale (which in my doctored bibliography becomes my first) and was reprinted by Terry Carr in his *The Best Science Fiction of the Year #8*.

And I've been story-doctoring in Kate Wilhelm's honor ever since.

One sentence on each please: Nisi Shawl, Colin Meloy, Star Trek, Dr. Johnson.

Nisi Shawl once washed my feet at a party, which deeply puzzled me; much later I realized that I should have been washing hers.

Colin Meloy is someone I had to look up because sometime in the early 2000s I stopped paying attention to rock music and filled the reclaimed cognitive space with jazz and audiobooks.

Star Trek is ultimately more of a force for good in SF, although very few fans realize why the transporter is murder.

I've been to Dr. Johnson's house, sat at his desk in his library, and thought about him but left no wiser than when I entered.

What is your favorite city? Why don't you live there?

New York, New York. I'm holding off on the move until my play is produced on Broadway.

My Jeopardy *answer: romantic comedy. You provide the question:*

What is the least understood genre?

You were on and once ran the New Hampshire Arts Council. How did that come about? What was it like?

My first involvement with the NH State Council on the Arts was when I applied to be on the Artists in the Schools roster. I was in the process of getting divorced and was casting around for a way to earn money to support my writing habit that didn't involve bagging groceries. I proposed to visit schools around the state to get kids to write and think about science fiction and the future. To do this I had to convince the council that a) I was an artist and b) I could teach. Back then in my experience writers and especially SF writers did not necessarily think of themselves as artists. Indeed, as I later learned, some arts councils in other states were turning SF writers down for roster spots for writing on the wrong side of the literary tracks. Not New Hampshire. I will admit that I learned to teach writing on the job. There were days when I waltzed in and was like Robin Williams in *Dead Poets Society* and others when I was like the saddest substitute teacher ever to lose control of a class. But I got better, and I liked the kids. I was actually getting more residency offers than I could accept when the professional staff approached me about serving on the council itself, which was composed of arts-friendly people from the business and non-profit communities, arts donors and a couple of working artists, one of whom was leaving. I was honored and said yes, so the governor nominated me. The councilors are something like a board of directors; we met monthly to oversee the professional staff, set policy and approve grants—all for no pay. I loved it! Part of the job was to travel around the state listening to artists and arts organizations and finding ways to help them connect with audiences. I was twice nominated to four-year terms on the council and in my last two years I was elected chair, which meant that I traveled to a number of national conferences representing our little state. I might still be on the council, had I not joined the faculty of the Stonecoast MFA program. There just wasn't time enough for both.

What I learned as a councilor is that the arts are destined ever to struggle in our capitalist system. The vast majority of artists are among the working poor and many worthy arts organizations regularly face economic ruin. What government support there is never balances the books.

Arts organizations try to make an argument for better and more reliable support by talking about the arts economy and its collateral benefits. Towns with an active theater community are more likely to have upscale restaurants and posh housing stock. Streets with art galleries tend to draw the Rolex crowd. There's merit to this, I suppose, but for me the best argument for supporting the arts is that they represent the soul of our culture. Alas, our soul does not fit into a cell on a spreadsheet.

What drew you into writing plays? The money or the fame?
Both. And still waiting.
I started writing plays by accident. Back in the day I was on the New Hampshire State Council on the Arts' Artists in Schools roster, which meant I traveled around the state talking about science fiction and fantasy and helping kids write stories. From 1989 to the early 2000s, I worked with K–12 kids in more than fifty NH schools and ate more bad lunches than I care to remember. Pizza day washed down with a carton of chocolate milk! American chop suey and a mealy apple! As an unexpected bonus, I was invited to join an ambitious theater residency with the goal of getting the students to write, stage, and present a new play to the community. It was a magical experience. My fellow artists gave me gentle nudges when I strayed off course, and in part because

of their expectations, and in part because of the kids' enthusiasm, we pulled it off. Word of what we accomplished traveled around the state and we did similar residencies around the state. After several, I tumbled to the notion that if seventh graders could write a creditable play with my help, I might be able to do it myself.

I started by adapting stories into one acts that got produced in local black box theaters. As you and I both know, it's kind of a thrill to sit in an audience that is enjoying your play. Some of my theater pals talked me into writing a couple of full-length historical plays. One was "I Have Not Yet Begun to Fight" about local NH hero John Paul Jones and featured an onstage battle between Jones's frigate *Bonhomme Richard* and the British *Serapis*. At one memorable performance, when the British captain called out at the climactic moment, "Sir, do you surrender?" the actor playing Jones blanked on his lines, replying simply, "No." Perhaps I should have taken that as an omen of how my theatrical career would go. But I did write another full-length play called "The Duel" which had a nice four-week run in two of the biggest theaters in the state. It was about the encounter between Hamilton and Burr but with an alternative history twist. This was long before Lin-Manuel Miranda's *Hamilton*. At the end of the first act, both duelists miss. In the second act, New England has seceded from the Union and the Civil War breaks out fifty years early, with Burr and Hamilton on opposite sides.

Since then I have limited myself to one acts and especially ten-minute plays, of which I've had maybe a dozen produced around the country.

You often teach writing. What's the hardest thing for people to learn? What's the easiest?

Endings are definitely the hardest and the most important. I'm no Isaac Asimov or Arthur C. Clarke, but I've always aspired to proclaim three laws of my very own. How about these? Jim's First Law: All great stories have great endings. Jim's Second Law: A story which reads great until its flawed ending is just an okay story. Jim's Third Law: A great ending will overshadow the flaws of a story which is otherwise just okay.

The easiest thing about writing is also the easiest to overlook. The only way to have a career as a writer is to send your stories out. Actually, this one isn't all that easy, because writers are good at finding reasons not to submit their work. Fear of rejection is the big one, but obsessive rewriting is almost as debilitating. As Valéry wrote, "A story is never completed, merely abandoned."

You do and sell Audible stories. How does that work?
I began reading aloud to my kids as a stay-at-home dad, classics like *Clifford the Big Red Dog* and *The Cat in the Hat*. When we graduated to the Oz series, I began to do voices. I remember casting the Wizard as a very broad W.C. Fields and the Scarecrow as Ernie from *Sesame Street*. As my career as a writer progressed, I was delighted to discover that fans at SF conventions would show up at readings to hear me pretend to be the characters in my stories. Readings are my favorite part of cons and I'm grateful to write in a literary community which honors them as a hallmark of its culture.

I'm kind of a gadget guy and I used to record my readings on cassettes and copy them for friends. When recordable CDs came along, I would run off dozens, some of which I sold but most of which I gave away at cons as promotion. But during the astonishing rise of the iPod and mp3s and podcasting and the downloadable audiobook, everything about recorded fiction changed. I was an early podcast adopter with my

Free Reads podcast, which featured me reading my backlist of published stories. But one of the smartest career moves I ever made was to talk Jacob Weisman at Tachyon Press into letting me record and podcast my standalone novella *Burn*, which he was about to publish. I posted a new chapter every week on *Free Reads*, and *Burn* got more than twenty thousand downloads in its first twelve months. I am convinced that it was the podcast rather than the print version that earned my novella its Hugo nomination and its Nebula win.

Meanwhile, *Free Reads* caught the attention of Steve Feldberg, who was keen to acquire SF for Audible.com. He approached me about transferring some of my *Free Reads* content to the Audible store and recording more of my stories. Lots more! Eventually I recorded and produced fifty-two short stories, novelettes and novellas for Audible, which were packaged into four collections or "seasons" under the titles of *James Patrick Kelly's StoryPod One*, *Two*, *Three*, and *Four*.

Alas, it was such a monumental task and the post-production took so much of my time, that I gave up my regular podcasts, both *Free Reads* and *StoryPod*, in part out of exhaustion. These days I mostly let the pros publish my works on audio, although I still get behind the microphone from time to time.

What kind of car do you drive?

My current set of wheels is a 2014 Honda CRV, but that is just quotidian transportation. My thrill rides have always had fewer than four wheels. In my twenties I itched for a motorcycle, but my wife at the time was adamantly opposed. Years passed—decades!—and in midlife I was musing about this forgotten two-wheel dream to my dear wife Pam Kelly when she shrugged and said she had no problems with motorcycles. I hadn't known this about her! Six months later, I swung my leg over my first bike, a Honda Rebel 250cc, which was fun but under-powered. Subsequently I moved up to Kawasaki Vulcan 400 and then to a Suzuki VStrom 600. A year ago, I decided that safety trumped buzz and made the jump to three wheels. My Can-Am Ryker 650cc is a trike with two wheels in the front and the drive wheel behind and a happy science fiction writer on the seat in between.

Do you ask Siri or use a map?
I have many thoughts about maps, all joyful. I never hesitate to ask Siri for directions and I always program long distance destinations into my car's GPS, if only to know when I'll arrive. On the other hand, I love to ride my motorcycle down back country roads until I am completely and gloriously lost. When I get home, I will then try to retrace my trip on Google maps. Google's satellite view, by the way, still feels like science fiction to me. I have spent happy hours peering at the Appalachian Mountain Club trail maps planning hikes for my wife and me to take. USGS topo maps fill me with delight. I have two historical maps hanging in my office and two more elsewhere in the house; I regard all of them as works of art.

I'm totally a map guy.

You and Kessel did a number of anthologies for Tachyon. How did that come about? How come I never made it into any of them?
Wait a minute! Your story "The Cockroach Hat" was in our *Kafkaesque*, pal.

I may misremember, but our editing gig probably started when I wrote my column about slipstream in *Asimov's Science Fiction*. In any event, Jacob Weisman somehow got the notion that I knew something about slipstream and floated the idea of an anthology. My first reaction was that I hadn't read widely enough to pick the right stories, and so after consulting John Kessel, we came back to Jacob with the idea that we would be coeditors. I note here that I regularly talk to Doctor Kessel about matters of business and craft, since he is far wiser and taller than I am. Our idea, for this and most of the subsequent anthologies, was that we would not only choose the tables of contents but that we would discuss the commonalities of the stories. We had arguments to make about slipstream, Franz Kafka, cyberpunk and postcyberpunk, and the singularity which we made in the introduction to each book. While some saw these books as attempts to establish a canon in various subgenres, we never did. We were just trying to provide context and start conversations around some wonderful stories and writers.

My personal favorite of these books was *The Secret History of Science Fiction* in which we sought to demonstrate that, purely in terms of craft and conceptualization, there was no appreciable difference between genre SF and the mainstream crossover SF. Because John and I have shared this core belief since we first started typing professionally, it was cathartic to make our case.

We had a great six-year run between 2006 and 2012 with these thesis anthologies. I'm not exactly certain why we stopped. Maybe it had something to do with Jacob passing on all the new ideas we pitched to him. Maybe it had something to do with the fact that editing was stealing time from our writing. Or maybe it was poetic justice for not including "Bears Discover Fire" either in *Feeling Very Strange* or *The Secret History*.

Three favorite SF movies? Three deplorables?
If I define "favorite" as films that influenced my thinking about our little corner of genre, I'd say *The Matrix* for its immersive VR, *Alien* for its

workers' spaceship, and *Galaxy Quest* for being the best Star Trek film ever. Of course, this list represents a cruel betrayal of the fanboy who grew up consuming the stale cheese of Creature Features. He wouldn't have hesitated to cite *Forbidden Planet*, the first and best *King Kong*, and *The Day the Earth Stood Still*, since he watched them over and over and over again. Because I sat uncritically through so many bad SF movies at an impressionable age, I now have very little tolerance for the deplorables in recent release. I have no use for most of the recent *Star Wars* products. I sat through *Interstellar* only because I was with friends and I saw maybe half of *Ad Astra* on a plane last year.

My True or False Question: True or False?
There are more things in heaven and Earth, Horatio / Than are dreamt of in your philosophy.

Did you read SF as a kid? What was the first story that lit you up?
I read all the SF in the children's section of my hometown library, especially the Two Toms (Tom Corbett and Tom Swift), often more than once. Then I asked the librarian's permission to cruise the adult stacks. (Fun fact: my pal Elizabeth Hand was probably just a few steps behind me. We grew up in the same town and have since compared notes about our many hours in that library.) So yeah, SF and I were not exclusive, but we dated heavily all through my teens. It's interesting, given my career as a short story writer, that I don't remember encountering any SF magazines until I got to college.

First story that lit me up? The truest answer here is *The Wizard of Oz*. Or rather all the Oz books, not only the L. Frank Baum novels but the sequels written by Ruth Plumly Thompson and John R. Neill. Is Oz SF? Well, I would argue that there is no robust definition of SF anymore, nor perhaps should there be. In the world I write in, SF now stands for speculative fiction and includes fantasy, horror, slipstream, weird fiction and on and on. But if I pretend that SF means stories about science or space or the future, then "A Planet Named Shayol" by Cordwainer Smith in *The Best of Sci-Fi 2*, edited by Judith Merril.

Our colleague Rachel Pollack once said, "Anyone who thinks guilt never helps anything has never been a writer." Was she onto something or just being a contrarian, as is often her wont?
As a survivor of an unrelenting Catholic education—kindergarten through college—I feel the shadow of guilt, earned and imagined, every day of my life. Not sure that it helps much, however.

Do you remember The Whole Earth Catalogue?
You realize that we date ourselves talking about such things, and SF is properly a young writers' genre, but of course I remember it! As I remember *Our Bodies, Ourselves*, *The Mother Earth News*, *The Electric Kool-Aid Acid Test*, Firesign Theatre, *Zap Comix*, *Hair*, and *Easy Rider*. How could I not? I was an eyewitness! I wrote "The First Law of Thermodynamics"!

The First Law of Thermodynamics

HE HAD DROPPED ACID maybe a dozen times, but had never forgotten his name before. He remembered the others—Cassie, Lance, Van—even though he'd left them waiting in the parking lot—when? A couple, ten minutes ago? An hour? Up until then, the farthest out he'd ever been was in high school, when he stared through the white on a sixty-watt bulb and saw the filament vibrating to a solo on Cream's "Sitting on Top of the World." It called to him in guitarese and he shrieked back. The filament said all life vibrated with a common energy, that we would exist only as long as our hearts beat to that indestructible rhythm. *Brang-brangeddy-brong, brang-brangeddy-brong*! Or something like. Actually, he might have been on mescaline the time the light bulb had played him the secret of the universe, or maybe it was Clapton, who was wailing back then like the patron saint of hallucinogens. But tonight his mind was well and truly blown by the blotter acid his new friends had called blue magic.

He wasn't particularly worried that he couldn't remember his straight name. He didn't feel at all attached to that chump at the moment, or to his dreary future. A name was nothing but a fence, closing him in. He was much happier now that the blue magic had transformed him into the wizard Space Cowboy, whose power was to leap all fences and zigzag through dayglo infinities at the speed of methamphetamine. Remembering the name on his student ID card was about as important as remembering the first law of thermodynamics. His secret identity was flunking physics and probably freshman comp too, which meant he wasn't going to last much longer at Notre Dame. And since his number in the draft lottery was fourteen, he was northbound just as soon as they booted him out of college—no way Nixon was sending *him* to Cambodia! So long, Amerika, hello Toronto. Or maybe Vancouver. New episodes in *The Adventures of Space Cowboy*, although he wasn't all that excited about picking snot icicles from his mustache. Lance said Canada would be a more happening country if it had beach front on the Gulf of Mexico.

He realized he had forgotten something else. Why had he come back to his room? Nineteen years old and his mind was already Swiss fucking cheese! He laughed at himself and then admired all the twisty little holes that were busy drilling themselves into the floor. The dull reality of the dorm emptied into them like soapy water swirling down a drain. The room reeked of Aqua Velva and Brylcreem, Balsinger's familiar weekend stink. *That's it*. Something to do with Balls, he thought. But his roommate was long since gone, no doubt sucking down quarts of Strohs while he told some Barbie doll his dream of becoming the world's most polyester dentist. Balls was the enemy; their room was divided territory, the North and South Viet Nam of Walsh Hall. Even when they were out, their stuff remained on alert. His pointy-toed boots were aimed at Balls's chukkas. Pete Townshend swung a guitar at Glen Campbell's head and *Zap Comix* blew cartoon smoke through the steamy windows of *Penthouse*. Now he remembered, sort of. He was supposed to borrow something—except the paint was melting off the walls. He picked the black cowboy hat off a pile of his dirty clothes, uncrumpled it and plunked it on. Sometimes the hat helped him think.

There was a knock. "Space?" Cassie peeked in and saw him idling at the desk. "Space, we're leaving."

It was Lance who had abridged his freak name—Lance, the wizard of words. Space didn't care; if someone he didn't like called him Space, he just played a few bars of Steve Miller's "Space Cowboy" in his head. Cassie he liked; she could call him whatever she wanted. In his opinion, Cassandra Demaras was the coolest chick who had ever gotten high. She stood almost six foxy feet tall and was wearing a man's pin-striped vest from Goodwill over a green tee shirt. Her hair was black as sin. Space lusted to see it spread across his pillow, only he knew it would never happen. She was a senior and artsy and Lance's. Not his future.

"Did you find it?" she asked.

"Ah . . . not yet," said Space cautiously. At least *someone* knew why he was here.

She stepped into the room. "Lance is going to split without you, man." Space had only joined the tribe last month and had already been left behind twice for stoned incompetence. "What's the problem?"

Her question was an itch behind his ear, so he scratched. She stared at him as if his skull were made of glass, and he felt the familiar tingle of acid telepathy. She used her wizardly powers to read his mind—what there was of it—and sighed. "The key, Space. You're supposed to be looking for what's-his-face's key."

"Balls." Suddenly he was buried in a memory landslide. They had been sitting around waiting for the first rush and Lance had been laying down this rap about how they should do something about Cambodia and how some yippies at Butler had liberated the ROTC building with balloons and duct tape, and then Space had started in about how Balsinger was at school on a work-study grant and had to put in twelve hours a week pushing a broom through O'Shaughnessy Hall, the liberal arts building, *for which he had the key*, and then everybody had gotten psyched so to impress them all Space had volunteered to lift the key, except in the stairwell he had been blown away by a rush so powerful that he'd forgotten who he was and what the hell he was supposed to be doing, despite which his body had continued on to the room anyway and had been waiting here patiently for his mind to show up.

Space giggled and said, "He keeps it in the top drawer."

Cassie went to Balls's desk, opened it and then froze as if she was peering over the edge of reality.

"What's he got in there now?" he asked, "Squid?"

As he came up behind her, he caught a telepathic burst that was like chewing aluminum foil. She was freaking out and he knew exactly why. This was where Balls kept his school supplies: a stack of blank three-by-five file cards held together with a red rubber band, scotch tape, a box of paper clips, six number 2 pencils with pristine erasers, six Bic ball points, a slide rule, an unopened bottle of Liquid Paper, and behind, loose-leaf, graph, and onionskin paper in perfect stacks. But it wasn't just Balls's stuff that had disturbed her. It was the way he had arranged everything, fitted it together with jigsaw-puzzle precision. In a world burning with love and napalm, this pinhead had taken the time to align pencils and pens, neaten stacks of paper—Space wouldn't have been surprised if he had reorganized the paper clips in their box. All this brutal order was proof that aliens from Planet Middle America had landed and were trying to pass for human! Space was used to Balsinger, but imagining the straightitude of his roommate's mind had filled Cassie with psychedelic dread.

"Space, are you as wasted as I think I am?" Her eyes had gone flat as tattoos.

"I don't know. What's the date?"

She frowned. "May 2, 1970."

"Who's president of the United States?"

"That's the problem."

He held up a fist. "How many fingers?"

She shook her head and was recaptured by the drawer.

The key to O'Shaughnessy Hall was next to the slide rule. Space picked it up and juggled it from one hand to another. It flickered through the air like a goldfish. This time when she glanced up, he bumped the drawer shut with his thigh. "Hey, remember what the dormouse said."

"No, I'm serious." She shook her head and her hair danced. "It's like time is breaking down. You know what I mean? One second doesn't connect to the next."

"Right on!" He caught the key and closed his fist around it.

"Listen! I've got to know where the peak is, or else I can't maintain. What if I just keep going up and up and up?"

"You'll have a hell of a view."

Maybe it was the wrong time for jokes. Space could see panic wisping off her like smoke. When he breathed it in, he got even higher. "Okay," he said "so the first wave is a mother. But I'm here and you're with me, so we'll just ride it together, okay?" He surfed an open hand toward her. "Then we groove."

"You don't understand." She licked her lower lip with a strawberry tongue. "Lance has decided he wants to score again, so we can trip all weekend. He's weirding me out, Space. My brains are already oozing from my fucking ears and he's looking for the next hit."

The blue magic was giving him a squirrely vibe; he thought he could feel a bad moon rising over this trip. Space had seen a bummer just once, back in high school, when a kid claimed he had a tiny Hitler stuck in his throat and thrashed around and drank twenty-seven glasses of water until he puked. Space had been paranoid that whatever monsters were chewing on the kid's brain would have him for dessert. But this kid—Space remembered him now—Lester Something, Lester was a pinched nobody who couldn't even tie his shoes when he was buzzed, not a wizard like Cassie or Lance or Space, with powers and abilities far beyond those of mortal men.

"Am I okay, Space?" She had never asked him for help before, put herself in his power. "What's going to happen to us?"

"We're going to have an adventure." Although he was worried about her, he was also turned on. He wanted to kiss his way through her hair to the pale skin on her neck. Instead he tugged at the brim of his hat. He was *Space Cowboy*. His power was that nothing could stop him, nothing could touch him. And so what if things were spinning out of control? That was the fun in doing drugs, wasn't it?

"Ready to cruise?" He beamed at her and was relieved to see his smile reflected palely on her face.

Somewhere in the future, a van honked.

#

"Say wonderful." Lance was giving Cassie orders.

The spooky moonlight spilled across the corn fields. Space glanced up from the floor of the van occasionally to see if the psychic ambience had improved any, but the lunar seas still looked like mold on a slice of electric bread.

"Wonderful," she said absently.

"No, mean it."

"Won . . . der . . . ful." Cassie's voice was a chickadee fluttering against her chest. Space knew this because she was wedged between him and Lance and they had their arms around her, crossing behind her back and over her chest, protecting her from lysergic acid diethylamide demons. He could feel her blood booming; her shallow breathing fondled his ribs. The Econoline's tires drummed over seams in the pavement as its headlights unzipped the highway at sixty-five miles an hour. He found himself listening to the world with his shoulders and toes.

"Full of wonder." Lance was smooth as an apple as he talked her down; his wizard power was making words dance. "I know, that can be scary, because you don't know where you're going or what you're going to find. Strangeness probably, but so what? Life is strange, people are strange. Don't fight it, groove on it." He squeezed her and Space took his cue to do the same. "Say you're a little girl at the circus at night and a clown comes up in the dark, and it's like *holy shit*, where's Mommy? But throw some light on him and you're laughing." He reached to flick on the overhead light. "See?"

It was the right thing to say because she blinked in the light and smiled, sending them flashes of pink cotton candy and dancing elephants and an acrobat hanging from a trapeze by his teeth. Space could feel her come spinning down toward them like a leaf. "Wonderful," she said, focusing. "I'll try."

Space was suddenly aware that his elbow was flattening her left breast and he was clutching Lance's shoulder. He shivered, let his arm slip down and wiped his sweaty palm on his jeans.

"Heavy, man," said Van. "You want to turn the light off before I miss the turn?" Van was at the wheel of his 1962 Ford Econoline van. It had a 144-cubic-inch, six-cylinder engine and a three-speed manual shift on the steering column and its name was Bozo. Van had lifted all Bozo's seats except his and replaced them with orange shag carpeting and a mattress fitted with a tie-dyed sheet. He had the Jefferson Airplane on the eight track; Grace Slick wondered if he needed somebody to love.

The answer was yes, thought Space. Yes, damn it! Lance was holding Cassie's hand. Van checked the rearview mirror, then braked, pulled off the highway and drove along the shoulder, craning his head to the right. Finally he spotted an unmarked dirt track that divided a vast and unpromising nothingness in two.

"Where the fuck are we?" said Space.

"We're either making a brief incursion into Cambodia," said Van, "or we're at the ass-end of Mishawaka, Indiana." Van had the power of mobility. He and Bozo were one, a machine with a human brain. No matter how stoned the world turned, Van could navigate through it. No one demanded poetry or cosmic truths from Van; all they expected of him was to deliver.

"Looks like nowhere to me."

"To the unenlightened eye, yes," said Lance. "But check it out and you'll see another frontier of human knowledge. Tripping is like doing science, Space. You can't just lounge around your room anymore listening to Joni Mitchell and dreaming up laws of nature. You have to go out into the field and gather data in order to grok the universe. Study the stars and ponds, turn rocks over, taste the mushrooms, smoke some foliage."

"Would someone take my boots off?" said Cassie.

"It's freezing, man," said Van. "Your feet will get cold." As Bozo bumped down the track, the steering wheel kept squirming in his hands like a snake.

"I've got cold feet already."

"Science is bullshit!" said Space. "Nothing but a government conspiracy to bring us down." He slid across the shag carpet and rolled the right leg of Cassie's jeans over an ankle-length black boot. "Like, if they hadn't passed the law of gravity, we could all fly."

Van laughed. "Maybe we could get Dicky Trick to repeal it."

"Somebody should repeal that asshole," said Cassie.

"Science is napalm," said Space. "Science is plastic. It's Tang." He eased her boot off. She was wearing cotton socks, soft and nubbly.

"It's the bomb," said Lance.

"Are we going to the farm?" Cassie wiggled her toes in Space's hand. "This is the way to the farm, isn't it?"

Her foot reminded him of the baby rabbit that Katie McCauley had brought for show-and-tell in the sixth grade; he hadn't wanted to put it down either. He pressed his thumb gently against her instep.

"You've never been to the farm, have you, Space?" said Lance. The road spat stones at Bozo's undercarriage.

"He's home," said Van. "I can see lights, man."

"Who?" Space said.

"Do you follow baseball?" Lance started to laugh.

The farm buildings sprawled across the land like a moonbathing giant. The barrel-chested body was a Quonset hut; a red silo arm saluted the stars. The weather-bitten face of the house was turned toward them; its narrow porch pouted. There were lights in the eyes, and much more light streaming from the open slider of the Quonset. Van parked next to a '59 Studebaker Lark that had been driven to Mars and back. He opened his door, took a deep breath of the night and disappeared.

"Oh, wow!" They could hear him scrabbling on the ground. "I forget how to walk," he said.

Space was the first to reach him. Van was doing a slow backstroke across the lawn toward the house. "For a moment there, man," he said, "I could've sworn I had wheels."

"Come on, you." Lance motioned Space to grab Van's shoulders and together they tried to lift him. "Get up." It was like stacking Jell-O.

"No, no, *no*." Van giggled. "I'm too wasted."

"I'm so glad you waited until now to tell us," said Lance. "How the hell do we get back to campus?"

"Oh, I'm cool to drive, man. I just can't stand up."

They managed to fold him back into the driver's seat and Cassie slapped Big Brother into the eight track. Space glanced over to the Quonset and saw a silhouette on the canvas of light framed by the huge open doorway. For a moment a man watched—no, *sensed* him. When he sniffed the air, something feathered against Space's cheek. Then the man ghosted back into the barn.

"Old Rog doesn't seem very glad to see us," said Lance.

The barn was fiercely lit—north of supermarket bright, just south of noon at the beach. The wildly colored equipment seemed to shimmer in the hard light. A golden reaper, a pink cultivator and a lobster-red baler were lined up beside a John Deere that looked like it had been painted in a tornado. The man had poked his head under its hood.

"Evening, Rog," said Lance. "Space, this is Roger Maris."

The man turned toward them; Space blinked. Roger Maris was wearing a pair of black jeans with a hole in the left knee and a greasy Yankee jersey over a gray sweatshirt. He stood maybe six feet tall and weighed a paunchy two hundred and change. He had that flattop crewcut, all right, and the nose like a thumb, but Space wasn't buying that he was Roger Maris. At least not *the* Roger Maris.

He'd been ten years old when Maris hit sixty-one home runs to break Babe Ruth's record, but in 1961 Space and his parents had been National League fans. They lived in Sheboygan and followed the Milwaukee Braves. Space's imagination had been more than filled by the heroics of Hank Aaron and Eddie Matthews; there was no room for damn Yankees. But then the Braves moved south in 1966 and Space had to accept the harsh reality that not only was God dead, but Warren Spahn was pitching in Atlanta. After that, he'd lost interest in baseball. He had no clue what had become of *the* Roger Maris since.

"Space?" Maris waved a socket wrench at him. "What the hell kind of name is Space?"

"Short for Space Cowboy," said Cassie.

Maris considered this, then put the wrench down, wiped his left hand on the pinstriped jersey and offered it to Space. "A hat don't make no cowboy," he said.

They shook. "A shirt don't make no ballplayer," said Space.

Maris's smile bandaged irritation. "What can I do you folks out of?" He gave Space a parting grip strong enough to crush stone.

"You got any more blue magic in your bag of tricks?" said Lance. "We're thinking of going away for the weekend."

"To where, Oz?" Maris shut his eyes; his lids were the color of the last olive in the jar. "Cowboy here ever done magic before?"

Now Space was annoyed; he was proud of his dope resume. "I've dropped Owsley, wedding bells and some two-way brown dot."

"Practically Ken Kesey." Cassie laughed. "And only a freshman."

"That shit's just acid," said Maris. "Magic goes deeper."

"He handled the first rush all right," said Lance. "We all did."

"You driving around with a head full of blue magic?" Maris frowned.

"Actually," said Lance, "Van's driving."

But Maris wasn't listening. He had closed his eyes again and kept them closed, his head cocked to one side as he received secret instructions from outer space. "It's your funeral," he said abruptly, and strode from the barn as if he'd just remembered he'd left the bath water running.

"I guess we scored." Lance shrugged. "Hey Rog, wait up!" He paused at the door of the Quonset, glanced uncertainly at Cassie and Space and then plunged after Maris.

"What does he mean, our funeral?" Cassie had turned the color of a Saltine.

"Don't ask me; I'm the rookie. Can't you see these training wheels on my head?"

"Deeper? Deeper than what?"

Space put his arm around her shoulder and led her from the Quonset into the baleful night.

#

Pacing Roger Maris's front parlor, Space remembered what Cassie had said about things getting disconnected. How could anyone deal acid and live in a place as square as a doctor's waiting room? The wallpaper was Midwestern Hideous: golden, flag-bearing eagles flapped between Civil War cannons on a cream field. If he stared long enough, the blue magic animated the pattern for him. Madness, *madness*—and Norman Mailer wondered why we were in Viet Nam! Lance and Cassie waited for Maris on a long, low, brown couch in front of an oval rug braided in harvest colors. Cassie watched the brick fireplace in which four dusty birch logs were stacked. Nearby, a television the size of a Shetland pony was tethered to the wall socket.

Space couldn't stand still. "Where did you dig this loon up?"

"He found us." Lance shot a quizzical look at Cassie. "After the Santana concert?"

She bit her lip and said, "Don't talk to me. I'm not here."

"Okay." Lance was teeth-grindingly patient. "That's cool."

By the door, a heavy brass pot was filled by a man's black umbrella and three baseball bats. "I mean, check this room," said Space.

Lance laughed. "I keep expecting Wally Cleaver to materialize and ask if I want to sniff some glue."

On waist high shelves beside a rocking chair were stacked a build-it-yourself Heathkit tuner, amp and turntable. Next to them was a rack of LPs. Space worried through them; they contradicted *everything* in the room. Maris had the rare nude version of John and Yoko's *Two Virgins*, *Weasels Ripped My Flesh* by the Mothers of Invention, Moby Grape, everything by Quicksilver Messenger Service, Dylan's *Blonde on Blonde*, the Airplane's *Surrealistic Pillow*.

"Look at this!" Space waved a copy of *Workingman's Dead* at Lance. "This is *not* Roger Maris—he's not anyone. His pieces don't fit together."

Lance pointed silently at a framed Western Union telegram that hung beside a painting of Guernseys.

MY HEARTIEST CONGRATULATIONS TO YOU ON HITTING YOUR 61ST HOME RUN. THE AMERICAN PEOPLE WILL ALWAYS ADMIRE A MAN WHO OVERCOMES GREAT PRESSURE TO ACHIEVE AN OUTSTANDING GOAL.
JOHN F. KENNEDY.

"So?" Space didn't know why it had become so important to him that this clyde wasn't the famous ballplayer. "He could've got this any-where—could've sent it to himself." Everything seemed so slippery all of a sudden; he felt a familiar twinge of dread. Just when he'd finally figured the world out, he was afraid he might have to stop believing in something. Again. This was exactly how it had felt when he given up on baseball, Catholicism, America, love, Star Trek, college. What was it this time? The only illusions he had left were that nothing mattered, that acid was wisdom and that he was a wizard.

He heard Maris on the stairs and skittered back to the couch next to Cassie, who was still elsewhere.

"A dozen hits of magic." Maris offered them a plastic baggie with a scatter of confetti clinging to the inside. Space took it. Each blotter was the size of a fingernail and was labelled with a blue ∞. "Sixty," said Maris.

Lance pulled two twenties and a joint from his tee shirt pocket. "Want to smoke?" He liked to close deals with some ceremonial pot. He said it was the Indian way, and also helped detect narcs. While he lit up, Space counted out a ten, a five and five ones, and put an empty wallet back in his jeans.

Lance passed the joint to Maris, who took an impatient toke.

"You said this is deeper than acid." Space jiggled the baggie. "What's that supposed to mean, anyway?"

Cassie twitched and returned from the dark side of the moon.

"You take a trip, you come back, nothing really changes." The smoky words curled out of his mouth. "This shit makes you become yourself faster, kind of hurries things along."

"Something wrong with that?" said Cassie.

"Depends on who you're supposed to be." Maris tucked the wad of money into his jeans. "But if I was you kids, I'd take the long way to the future." He offered her the joint; she waved it over to Space.

"Sounds like Timothy Leary bullshit to me." Space took a deep, disgusted pull and immediately regretted it. Lance's pot tasted like electrical fire; it was probably laced with Mr. Clean.

"Timothy Leary's dead," sang Lance. "So if I'm not myself, who am I? Marshall McLuhan? Abbie Hoffman?"

"You're faking it, that's what being young is all about. When you're young, there ain't all that much of you, so you pretend there's more."

"Hell, you're the one preten—" Space couldn't hold it in anymore; he was racked by a fit of coughing.

"Space," said Cassie.

"You never hit sixty-one homers." Space gasped; his head felt like it was filling with helium. "I bet you've never even been to Yankee Stadium."

Maris's face was hard as the Bible. "You want to see my license, Cowboy?" In the uneasy silence, he fetched an ashtray from the hi-fi shelf. "Me, I stayed young a long time, mostly because I never did nothing but play ball. Growing up ain't something they really encourage in the bigs. When I got traded to the Yankees, I was just the kid who was going to play right field next to Mantle. I was MVP that season, '60." Talking about baseball seemed to calm him. He took another drag, ashed the joint and then offered it again to Cassie.

"Mantle?" This time she puffed politely.

"Mickey Mantle played center field," said Lance. "Tell them about the home run." Space wasn't sure whether Lance really believed or was egging Maris on for a goof.

"That was the next year, when me and Mick hit all the homers. Only he got sick and I still didn't have the record on the last day of the season. We were playing the Red Sox at the Stadium. By then a lot of people had given up, probably thought I didn't have sixty-one in me. I remember it was a cool day but real bright, the sun beating down on all the empty seats. The fans who showed were jammed into the right field stands, just in case. The Sox started Tracy Stallard, a righty, fastball pitcher. I flied out to Yaz in the first but when I came up in the fourth . . ."

The contours of his body changed, as if the weight of the last nine years had fallen away.

"He started me with two balls away. Then the third pitch, he made a mistake, got too much of the plate. I was always a mistake hitter. I got a real good cut at it and then . . . I just stood and watched. It landed near the bullpen, about ten rows into the stands, people scrambling after it. There was a fog of noise; it was like I couldn't find my way around the bases. When I got back to the dugout, Blanchard and Skowron and Lopez wouldn't let me in, they were blocking the top step, making me go back out into the noise. That was the problem, I couldn't never find my way out of that god-damned noise."

"Is that why you left baseball?" asked Cassie

"Nah." Maris closed his eyes again; he was definitely listening to *something*. "Nah, it's 'cause I ain't a kid anymore." Suddenly he looked spent; Space could see a looseness under the chin. "I'm thirty-six years old."

"That's still pretty young," said Cassie.

"Well then, there's this." He rolled up the gray sweatshirt, uncovering his left forearm. A scar, smooth and white as the belly of a snake, sliced from the ball of his thumb up toward the elbow. "The VC likes to rig these homemade mines, see. Couple of fragmentation grenades with the spoons attached to a tripwire. Me and Luther Nesson were walking point outside of Da Lat and the poor bastard stepped into one. Died in a splatter and left me a souvenir. A chunk of shrapnel chewed on my palmaris longus muscle and severed a couple of tendons."

Space contemplated the wound with vast relief; for a moment back there, Maris had almost convinced him. Now he felt a grudging admiration for Maris's creativity, his devotion to detail, the weight of his portrayal—the man had elevated *lunacy* to an *art*. And of course the Nam angle made it all the more poignant. Space imagined that, if he had seen what Maris had seen, he might well be strumming a ukulele and warbling like Tiny Tim.

"Bummer." Lance stubbed the roach out and took the baggie. "Hey, we better go check on Van, make sure he didn't float away." He stood. "So anyway, thanks, man." He reached for Cassie's hand.

"What's happening?" Cassie scooted away from him and bumped into Space. "We're going already? What about the rest of the story?"

Maris waved at the parlor. "Sister, you're looking at it."

Outside, Van was amusing himself by flashing a light show against the side of the farmhouse while he sang along to *Sergeant Pepper*. *High beam-low beam-right blinker-off-low beam-left blinker*. ". . . the *girl* with ka*lei*doscope *eyes*." He had a voice like a loose fan belt.

Maris followed them onto the porch and watched, flickering in the headlights. As Cassie ducked into Bozo, Maris called out. "Cowboy! How much you want for the hat?"

"Huh?"

"Pay no attention," Lance hissed. "Just get in."

"It's not for sale." Space stepped away from Bozo.

"Sixty bucks says it is."

Space tugged at the brim; he had almost forgotten he was wearing it. He started back toward Maris. It wasn't much of a hat—Space had stepped on it many times, spilled Boone's Farm Apple Wine on it, watched as one of Lenny Kemmer's Winstons had burned a hole in the black felt crown. "Is this some kind of joke?"

Van killed the lights and Beatles. Lance and Cassie deployed on either side of Bozo.

Maris came to the top of the porch steps. "You got doubts," he said. "You think I've been shitting you all night."

When Space tried to deny it, his tongue turned to peanut butter.

"Hell, Cowboy, you don't believe in nothing."

"So?"

"So I want to buy the hat." Maris came down the first step. "For a experiment." Second step. "And you gotta help." Bottom step. "Sixty." He unfolded the wad of bills and thrust them at Space.

"Hey, Rog," said Lance. "He's just a kid. Leave him alone."

Abraham Lincoln gazed up at Space, appraising the quality of his courage.

"What kind of experiment?" said Cassie.

"Scientific. Cowboy and me are going to measure something."

Space nipped the money without speaking and offered Maris the hat.

Maris clapped him on the shoulder. "You just hold onto that for now." He turned Space toward the Quonset. "See that barn? How far would you say it is?"

As Space peered into night, the Quonset receded and then flowed back toward him. "I don't know. Fifty, sixty feet?"

"More like a hundred, but that's okay. Now you're gonna stand in that doorway and get a good tight grip on the brim." He raised Space's arm. "Hold it to one side, just like that. Arm's length."

"Space." Cassie slipped between them. "Give him back his money and let's get out of here."

Maris brushed past her and surveyed the shrubbery along the porch. He poked by a couple of crewcut yews, a rhododendron in bud, a forsythia already gone by.

Cassie kept insisting. "Time to *go*, man." Like she was his mother.

The edge of the garden was defined by a row of smooth beach stones, painted white. Maris knelt with a grunt and hefted one the size of a peach, only flatter and more egg-shaped.

"Everyone remembers me for the homers, but I could play the field too." He brushed dirt off the stone. "Won a Gold Glove, you know. Didn't nobody stretch a single on Roger Maris."

"Jesus God," said Cassie, "what are you morons trying to prove? That your balls are bigger than your brains?"

That summed it up nicely, thought Space. Maris was playing a testosterone game with his head. Space was at once a creature of the game and a spectator. A poor nervous physics major sat in the stands, watching in horror, while Space Cowboy was grooving on a Grade A adrenaline high. And why not? He was a nineteen-year-old wizard whose power was that nothing could touch him, nothing could stop him. He looked over at Lance, who was pale as the moon. "Right *on!*" Space said.

He counted the paces off: *thirty-nine, forty, forty-one.* Forty-two to the Quonset's open doorway—figure three feet to a pace, so let's see, three times two was six and three times four was twelve—was that right? He had won his high school's Math Medal back in the Pleistocene. A hundred and twenty-six feet was just about the distance from third base to first. He bowed, flourished the hat to Cassie and then held it up in his moist, outstretched hand.

Maris turned at a right angle to the Quonset; he held the stone behind him, just off the hip. He scowled at the hat over his front shoulder and then paused. He shut his eyes and listened to the howl of the Dog Star long enough for a bead of sweat to dribble from Space's arm pit. Then Maris nodded, reared back and strode quickly forward—*open your eyes, goddamnit!* His arm snapped past his ear and the stone came screaming at Space like the headlamp of God's own Harley—or maybe it was Space who screamed, he couldn't tell, he couldn't move, his entire future had collapsed into an egg-shaped stone and time stopped and for an eternity he thought *what a fucking waste* and then time resumed with a sneeze and the hat spun him halfway around but he held on to it and something *thwocked* against the concrete floor of the Quonset and again, *thwocka-thwocka-thwok*! For a moment there was utter silence, which drummed in his ears like the finale of the 1812 Overture. Space whispered, "Out of sight," and giggled. Then he shouted so the others could hear. "OUT OF SIGHT!"

Space was surprised that the stone hadn't ripped off the top of the hat but instead had come through the pinch on the front side, leaving a hole big enough for Lance to put his fist through. Lance handed it to Van who offered it to Cassie who wanted no part of it. "Are you boys about through?" Her voice was a fistful of nails.

"Yeah," said Lance. "Time to cruise."

Van brought the hat to Maris, who was kneading his biceps. Maris stared right through him. "See what magic can do, Cowboy?" His smile had no teeth in it. "You can make yourself into a star, if that's who you're supposed to be."

"Mr. Maris," said Space, opening his wallet. "How much for that hat?"

#

Van, Space and Lance staggered out of Kresge's and across the parking lot, laughing. The cashier had rung up the eight cans of Rust-Oleum—two each of red, yellow, green and black—the one pound bag of Fritos, the four Almond Joys, the six packages of Fun Tyme Balloons, the dozen rolls of crepe ribbon, the two packs of Teaberry gum and then, as the register stuck out its paper tongue at her, she had asked them who the party was for. When Lance had said, "President Nixon, ma'am," she was so transparently croggled that it was all Space could do to keep from dropping to his belly and barking like a seal.

Cassie, who had been waiting for them in Bozo, didn't see what was so funny, but then she hadn't eaten that second blotter of blue magic, either. Ken Kesey and the Merry Pranksters had a saying: you were either on the bus or off. Space was no telepath, but it occurred to him that Cassie might be about to stand up and pull the signal cord for her stop.

"She's probably calling the cops on us right now," Cassie said.

"For what, indecent composure?" said Lance. "Chortling in a No Humor Zone?"

"How about possession? You've got Space here mooning around in a cowboy hat with a frontal lobotomy and you two are so wasted you're tripping over gum spots on the parking lot." She shook her head. "You guys are dangerous, you know that?"

"Only to ourselves." Van swerved Bozo around an oncoming Vega and roared onto the highway, headed back toward campus. "Break out the chips."

They crunched to themselves for a few moments. Space was glad that Cassie was no longer freaking out, only now she had turned so fucking sensible that she was stretching his nerves. They were tripping, *ferchrissakes*; this was no time to be responsible. "How about some tunes?" he said.

Van turned on the radio.

. . . of student protests continued today in the wake of President Nixon's decision to send troops into Cambodia. In Maryland, Governor Marvin Mandel has put the National Guard on alert after two days of unrest on the campus . . .

"I said tunes!" Space leaned forward to punch a selector button.

"Shh, listen." Lance yanked him back.

And at Kent State University in Ohio, a fire of undetermined origin swept through the ROTC building this evening. Firemen responding to the blaze were hampered by students throwing rocks and cutting hoses.

"Hey, man," said Van. "Maybe we should go after ROTC too."

"Earlier today, a group of two thousand students marched through downtown Kent, prompting local officials to order a dawn-to-dusk . . ."

"No," Lance said. "That's where they'll be expecting trouble. Besides, we've got the key to O'Shag."

"This whole gig is bogus." Cassie nudged the paper K-Mart sack with her boot. "It's not going to accomplish anything, except maybe get us arrested."

"Hey, we're going wake up this fucking campus," Space said.

"Fucking ay!" said Van.

"Shake the jocks out of their beds."

"Right on, man, right on!" Van pumped his fist.

"Light a fire under old Hesburgh."

"Tell it, brother!" Van leaned on the horn.

"Lay off, you guys," said Lance. "Cassie, you heard the radio. People all over the country are protesting. We've got a chance to make a statement here."

"With balloons and spray paint?"

"Better than guns and bombs." Lance rested his hand on her knee. "You thought it was cool before."

"That wasn't me, that was the acid."

Turning to sports, Dust Commander has won the Kentucky Derby. A fifteen-to-one shot . . .

She rested her cheek against the window. "Look, I'm going to graduate in a couple of weeks. I'm too old to be playing Wendy to your Lost Boys. Maybe I should just go back to the dorm and crash."

And in the American League, the Angels beat the Red Sox, 8-4, it was the Yankees 7, the Brewers 6 . . .

Space fingered the hole in his hat and wondered if he had it in him to be a star.

#

Van sauntered toward the main entrance to O'Shaughnessy Hall. The liberal arts building was one of largest and ugliest on campus, a stack of four Gothic Revival ice cube trays with a yellow brick veneer. Cassie, Space and Lance watched from the chill shadows as Van waltzed innocently up to the door, tried it as if he'd expected O'Shag to be open at 11:34 on a Saturday night, shrugged and cruised on.

"Of course, if it wasn't locked, we wouldn't be breaking and entering." Cassie made no effort to keep her voice down. "Jerry Rubin would have to take points off."

Lance had used his wizard power to talk Cassie into sticking with them, but Space wasn't sure it had been his swiftest move of the evening. Doubt was contagious, especially when your feet were wet. They had left Bozo in student parking and stolen across the tidy greens of the campus, weighting their shoes with spring dew. The night was getting colder; Space could see his breath plume. He ground his teeth to keep them from chattering. It took Van forever to circle back to them.

They slunk around to O'Shag's smaller north entrance, checking for any signs of activity inside. The classrooms were all dark but that didn't mean some English professor might not be late-nighting in one of the windowless offices, slugging Jim Beam and writing poems about English professors for the *Dead Tree Review*. This time the others stayed behind while Space approached the door, clutching Balls's key. It wasn't until he was fitting it into the lock that he realized there might be an alarm. He looked back at the others in a panic but they were no help. Neither were the stars, some of which were flashing blue like the cherry on a cop car. He could almost hear the Pleiades shrilling at him as he tried to turn the key to the right. It wouldn't budge. He thought the moon's alarm would sound deeper and more reproachful, like a foghorn. He turned the key left and the dead bolt clicked. *Moon, spoon, you fucking loon*. He pushed against the door and it swung open, dumping him into O'Shaughnessy Hall.

He went through a dimly lit stairwell to the long, dark hall of the first floor. The block walls on either side were pierced by wooden doors. Space could not make out the far end. Although he had passed this way every Monday, Wednesday and Friday for eight months, Space felt lost. The place he knew and hated teemed with sound and light and bodies. This one was empty, silent as a dream and all the doors were closed, creating an odd pressure in the hall, as if the building were holding its breath.

He heard a door tick open, a squeak of sneakers against the rubber mat in the stairwell, the whisper of corduroy pants. Lance said that the reason Van always wore corduroys was that he needed more texture in his life.

"In here," said Space.

"No lights?" Van peered .

"No."

They joined Lance and Cassie in the stairwell. Lance knelt in a corner of the stairwell and handed out supplies from the K-Mart bag. "We'll each take a floor," he said. "Fifteen minutes and out."

"But what should we say, man?" asked Van.

"Like I said, just make a statement," said Lance. "It's your life and their war."

Cassie waved off a package of balloons. "Keep the party favors." She went up the stairs with a can of Rust-Oleum in each hand.

"Bring the empties back and no fingerprints, okay?" said Lance. "Fifteen minutes—let's do it!" He and Van took the stairs two at a time.

Space sprayed a blue peace sign on the door to Room 160 but was strangely unconvinced by it. Then what kind of statement did he have in him? He immediately regretted the *fuck Nixon*; it was obvious as air. *Hell no, we won't go* sprawled the entire length of Room 149 and came to a disappointing conclusion on 147. Room 141 read *Out now*. He took a balloon from of his pocket, blew it up and almost fainted but managed to hold it pinched between thumb and forefinger. Out of where? Cambodia? Viet Nam? Notre Dame? Instead of tying the balloon, Space let it go and it leapt, hissing, from his hand. He wrote *revolution* on the east wall, *make love not war* on the west, then left them to futile debate. He was now deep into the hall; the visibility was less than a class in either direction. He could feel the future watching as he wrote *acid test* on Room 133. Pale secondhand moonlight glimmered through the tall wire-reinforced glass slits in each door. 125 said, *God is dead.* Long red runs dribbled from the "o" in *God*, like blood from the crown of thorns. Was proclaiming the demise of the deity a political statement? *Maris 61/61* on 117. That would leave the campus fuzz scratching their balls even though Old Rog had proved that it was cool to *talk the talk*, man, just as long as you can *walk the walk*. But Space still couldn't see the end of the fucking hall.

At that moment, something splatted on his cheek. Space swiped at it, thinking it might be his own sweat. The finger came away dry; he could feel his skin tighten in fear. *Pa-chuk.*

"Hey!"

Pa-chuk, pa-chuk. The two drops hit his left arm like marbles on a snare drum and he spun wildly away. *Pa-chuk.* Space moaned and started to run. A phantom storm in the middle of O'Shaugnessey Hall was hairy enough, but these weren't just polite raindrops. They were big and cold and rude as eggs. *Pa-chuk*.

And this was it, he realized: the bummer he had helped Cassie dodge was seething all around him and he knew he had to get out, get *out*, that he had been wandering blindly and without purpose down this hallway ever since he had come to Notre Dame *papa-chuk* but he could no longer go back to his parents and Sheboygan and Cathy, that lying bitch *pa-chuk* but there was no sense in going any farther because the hallway stretched on to some distant and unknowable infinity and besides, he had to get the hell out, which was when the doors began to vibrate and the light of insight came knifing through the long, thin windows and he saw the hall with the same acid clarity with which he had heard the filament of a sixty-watt bulb riffing about the mysterious energy that abided in all life, only now he could sense a new secret *papa-chuk*: that there was no future in wandering down an empty hall, that in order to find his life he would have to choose where to expend his energy. Pick a door, *damn it*. Room 110 was right in front of him, but it was even and Space knew he had to be odd. He about-faced; nothing could stop him. The doorknob of 109 was warm as a kiss.

Space put a hand to his forehead to shield his eyes. Sunlight poured through windows which framed snow-covered mountains. The sky was the blue of heaven; the snow on the ground glistened. He had entered a classroom all right, but it obviously wasn't in the same corner of reality as South Bend, Indiana.

A balding man stood behind the head desk and typed with two fingers—the teacher, Space assumed. He was wearing suede cowboy boots, black pants, a denim work shirt buttoned to the neck and—*holy shit*, the dude had a gold earring!

He did not seem to notice Space.

Neither did the students now filing in behind him. They seemed too young to be in college; they had that stunned glaze of high school seniors—except that some of them had tattoos. The sides of one girl's head had been shaved to a gunmetal shadow. A boy in a flannel shirt had on the flimsiest headphones Space had ever seen; they were attached to a transistor radio hooked to the kid's belt. *Walkman*—the word sprang unbidden to his mind. *Walk the walk*, man.

Space's first instinct was to bolt from the room, or at least slouch like a student behind a desk in the back, but instead he approached the teacher. As he got closer he saw that the squashed typewriter had no paper in it, that it wasn't any kind of machine Space had ever seen before, but then there was another strange word melting on his tongue like a lifesaver—*laptop*. It was a funny word and he might have laughed, except that he had by now come too close to the teacher, close enough so that he could wiggle his toes inside the man's boots, so close that he could jingle the keys to an '88 Dodge Caravan in his front pants pocket and, in the back pocket, feel the bulk of a wallet not-quite-filled with thirty-eight dollars and a NatWest Visa card with an unpaid balance of $3,734.80 on which he was paying a 9.9 percent APR and a California driver's license and a picture of a pretty little blonde girl named Kaitlin, so impossibly close that he could feel the weight of a single gold band around the fourth finger of his left hand and remember Judy's breath feathering against his neck after she kissed him goodbye that morning.

The bell rang and the class came to what passed for attention at Memorial High.

"Good morning, people." He turned to the board and scrawled, *1st law of thermodynamics* in handwriting which was almost as legible as an EKG scan. He faced the class again. "Can anyone tell me what this is?"

He was astonished to see Ben Strock with his hand up. Most days the kid sat looking as if he had just been hit in the head with a shovel, even though he *was* pulling down a B+. "Yes, Ben?"

"Uh . . . bathroom pass, Mr. Casten."

Jack Casten waved him from the room. "Anyone else?"

Of course, Feodor Papachuk raised his hand. *Fucking suck-up,* thought the part of Jack Casten that was still Space Cowboy and always would be. "Go ahead, Feodor."

"The first law of thermodynamics," said Feodor Papachuk, "is that energy can neither be created or destroyed but may be changed from one form to another."

Donut Hole

Characters: Tonya, a medical technician
                     Emily, a psychiatric technician
                     Manny, a patient

Time: the future
Setting: a re-bodying lab

At rise: Emily is working on unconscious Manny. He is stretched across three or four chairs and is hidden from the audience by a sheet.

Emily knocks and enters.
EMILY: Sorry I'm late. The tube was a zoo . . . What the hell?
TONYA: Relax, it's only an eyeball.
EMILY: On the floor?
TONYA: I dropped it.
EMILY: You dropped an eyeball?
TONYA: They're kind of slippery. Pick it up?
EMILY: What? With my hands?
TONYA: If you don't mind.
EMILY: I do mind. I told you I'd be here—why didn't you wait?
TONYA: They delivered that damaged brain so I had to finish building him. The clock was ticking.

EMILY: (*picks up the eyeball gingerly*) Sterilizer or trash?

TONYA: Five minute rule. Sterilizer.

EMILY: (*deposits it*) Now what?

TONYA: Pop another eyeball in, would you? I've got to keep this brain seated until the spinal cord fuses to the stem.

EMILY: Where?

TONYA: Cooler. Second drawer on the left.

EMILY: (*opens it*) Nope. Tongues.

TONYA: Your other left.

EMILY: Got it. (*inserts eyeball, inspects Manny*) You have been busy. (*uncovers Manny, out of sight*) Wow, primary sexual characteristics too?

TONYA: Yeah, well, the time factor. Time to get him powered up, see how much of his mind came through the scan.

EMILY: Didn't do him any favors down there.

TONYA: Everything is to scale. He won't complain. They never do. (*steps back*) Done.

EMILY: (*checks tablet*) Yep. Brain has just begun the handshake with the new body. Close the skull?

TONYA: Do it. I'll set the paddles.

EMILY: Spray some damn clothes on him first. If he wakes up naked, he might start dissociating.

TONYA: Right. (*does this then sets paddles*) Initial pulse 2,000 volts at 20 microseconds.

EMILY (*enters data on tablet*) Biphasic shock 2,000 volts. Duration 20. Clear.

(*paddles fire SFX. Manny grunts.*)

EMILY: A spike of consciousness, then flat. More juice?

TONYA: 3,000 volts, same duration.

EMILY: Clear.

(*paddles fire SFX*)

MANNY: (*gives an inarticulate cry, sits upright*) Oh, shit. (*sees the two techs*) Really? Uploaded?

TONYA: Afraid so.

MANNY: How did it happen . . . I mean that I'm here?

EMILY: You're supposed to tell us.

MANNY: (*dazed*) And this . . . this isn't really me. (*examines himself*) A different body.

TONYA: Brand new. Still on warranty.

EMILY: So you're not surprised?

MANNY: No, I guess I'm not.

TONYA: That's a good sign.

MANNY: How long?

EMILY: Only a couple of days. We started building you Tuesday?

TONYA: I was here Monday. Where were you?

MANNY: No. How long was I . . . gone?

TONYA: Dead, you mean?

EMILY: Technically he wasn't dead.

TONYA: Technically is just a word.

EMILY: They got the brain out in time.

TONYA: And froze it.

EMILY: Frozen, right.

TONYA: As in not alive. Technically.

MANNY: It was my birthday. It's hazy but I remember Mina was there. Our kids.

EMILY: So you have a name? For yourself, I mean.

MANNY: Of course I have a name.

(*they wait*)

MANNY: It'll come to me.

EMILY: (*enters data on tablet*) Time to stand you up. Get that brain talking to all your new parts.

MANNY: Right. (*He is shaky; the techs help him up*) What's that music?

EMILY: You hear music?

TONYA: What kind of music?

MANNY: (*listens*) Like that. Tell me you don't hear that? (*hums a tune*)

TONYA: Damage to the auditory cortex?

EMILY: Maybe just tinnitus. (*scans him with tablet*) Some kind of feedback?

TONYA: Don't ask me. You've got the instrument.

MANNY: I'm here, you know. And there's definitely music. (*listens*) No, it's gone.

TONYA: Good.

EMILY: You mentioned a name. Mina.

MANNY: My wife.

EMILY: And kids? Your birthday?

MANNY: March 19. Leonard and . . . and the girl . . . cute little girl.

EMILY: What color is her hair?

(*Manny shakes his head.*)

TONYA: (*offers to shake his hand, trying to take him by surprise*) I'm sorry, sir, I don't believe I caught your name.

MANNY: It's like pieces of me are missing. How long is that supposed to last?

EMILY: Everybody's different. We'll call you Manny for now.

MANNY: No, that's not my name. I know that for sure.

TONYA: It's an annoyance prompt, Manny. Standard procedure in these cases. You'll get tired of hearing it and then you'll remember your real name.

MANNY: I'm already tired. I need to sit down.

EMILY: No, no, no. Your new body doesn't get tired. You're done with tired, Manny.

TONYA: Can you stand on your own? (*steps away*)

MANNY: (*sways, catches himself*) I think so.

EMILY: Good. Then we're going to ask you to do some simple exercises, Manny.

TONYA: First, arms outstretched to the sides. Good. Now touch your nose with your pinky. Left. Your other left. Pinky, Manny. Good. Right, pinky to nose.

MANNY: Do I know your names? We haven't met before, have we?

EMILY: Very good, Manny. (*enters data*) We've been waiting for you to ask. Shows progress. I'm Emily, she's Tonya.

MANNY: Okay. And you do what, exactly?

TONYA: We're the team who built you. I specialize in this (*pokes him in the chest*) and she specializes in this. (*taps his temple*) Now that we've finished your uploading, we check our work.

EMILY: And help you. Adjust, you know. Understand.

MANNY: I don't understand what we're doing here. What happened to me? Why can't I remember anything?

EMILY: (*steps back to create distance; uses tablet to scan Manny*) Walk over to me, would you Manny?

TONYA: Go ahead.

    (*Manny stumbles, catches himself, walks painfully to Emily, who catches him*)

TONYA: (*increasing the distance*) Now back to me.

    (*Manny does better this time. Skips on the last step*)

TONYA: Nice work. What's four times seven?

MANNY: Twenty-eight.

EMILY: What planet is between Jupiter and Neptune?

MANNY: Saturn.

TONYA: Name any play by Shakespeare.

MANNY: *Macbeth.*

EMILY: You're supposed to call it "the Scottish play."

MANNY: I'm not superstitious.

TONYA: I think he's ready. Let's try it.

EMILY: Manny, do you know what proprioception is?

MANNY: Something about moving around? Knowing where you are?

EMILY: Where your body is in space. Very good. We want you to do a proprioception exercise. Your wife, Mina.

MANNY: What about her?

EMILY: Did you two ever dance?

MANNY: Dance?

TONYA: (*opens her arms*) Don't mind if I do. (*pulls Manny to her, places his arms around her. They dance awkwardly.*)

MANNY: This is silly. There's no music.

TONYA: Hum a few bars and we'll fake it.

> (*Manny hums some familiar tune. Tonya and Emily pick it up. They dance for maybe a minute and Manny's movement becomes more fluid. Once they get in sync, Emily calls out a question, waits for an answer and resumes humming.*)

EMILY: What's the green stuff in plants called?

MANNY: Chlorophyll.

EMILY: Chocolate or vanilla?

MANNY: Pistachio.

EMILY: How do you take your coffee?

MANNY: Cream, two sugars.

> (*Manny spins Tonya*)

EMILY: Who are you dancing with, Manny?

MANNY: Umm.

TONYA: What's your name?

(*Manny stops to think*)

EMILY: (*stops humming*) That's it, then. Done.

MANNY: It'll come to me.

TONYA: No, it won't.

MANNY: But I was almost there.

EMILY: If it doesn't happen in the first ten minutes, it never happens.

MANNY: It? What are you talking about?

EMILY: Listen, Manny. Each individual has something unique . . .

TONYA: Not the donut again.

EMILY: . . . at the center of all our memories. An identity that draws everything we know together. I'm sorry, but it looks like your center didn't make the transition when you uploaded.

MANNY: This is crazy. I'm talking to you and you're talking to me.

TONYA: We're talking to you. Something is talking back to us and we're not exactly sure what it is.

MANNY: This isn't happening. Are you even real?

(*Tonya slaps him*)

TONYA: What do you think? Was that real?

MANNY: Okay. So I'm a donut. So what?

EMILY: You decide whether you want to live with that or not.

MANNY: Or not?

TONYA: Some think not is best.

MANNY: You're going to kill me, is that it? I flunked your test, so I'm nothing. Expendable Manny, that poor bastard nobody.

EMILY: Kill isn't right word, technically. (*hands him the tablet*) But there is an off switch.

MANNY: And people actually do this? Turn off?

TONYA: You'd be surprised.

MANNY: What if I don't want to? (*tries to give the tablet back, they refuse it*)

EMILY: Then don't. Your decision.

MANNY: That can't be right. I can just walk out that door?

TONYA: Stay here for as long as you need to figure things out. Then, whatever.

MANNY: Stay here and do what? Live? There's no food.

TONYA: You don't eat anymore.

EMILY: He can eat. He just doesn't need to. But we should go.

TONYA: You need to be alone. You have a lot to think about. You have a very nice body there.

EMILY: Tonya did a great job.

TONYA: You helped.

EMILY: I'll take lead next time, okay? I need to work on my anatomy skills. I'll leave the flat extra early.

TONYA: That body will last you a long time.

EMILY: And the hardware up there works fine. (*taps Manny's head*) It's strictly a software glitch. You could use that brain to become someone, Manny. Fill in the center. But it won't be who you were.

EMILY: Hey, if you decide to leave, would you mind turning out the lights?

(*They exit*)

MANNY: So I'm a glitch. (*picks up the tablet*) Manny the glitch. Manny, Manny, Manny. (*dances and sings his name for several beats*) Shit, my name isn't Manny. (*slows and stares into the tablet*) Stop. (*stops moving*) How about Lawrence? (*tentatively, puts tablet aside*) Lawrence. It has a kind of music. (*thinks it over and is pleased*) Lawrence!

blackout

Who Owns Cyberpunk?

Origin Story

In the beginning, nobody could decide what to call the cyberpunks. Various names were proposed: Radical Hard SF, the Outlaw Technologists, the Eighties Wave, the Neuromantics, and the Mirrorshades Group. You can see the problem. For a movement to catch on, it needs a catchy name. In 1983, a writer named Bruce Bethke had published a story called "Cyberpunk" in the November issue of *Amazing Stories*. But although he can claim the original coinage, Bethke did not exercise his naming rights. Editor Gardner Dozois is generally credited with popularizing the term. Here he is, writing in 1984, "About the closest thing we have to a self-willed aesthetic school, would be that group of writers, purveyors of bizarre hard-edged high-tech stuff, who have on occasion been referred to as 'cyberpunks'" (Dozois, 1985, 11).

Of course, the first cyberpunks were less a "self-willed aesthetic school," and more a group of ambitious, like-minded, American baby boomers who read and liked each other's work. Mostly writers at the beginning of their careers, their influence on one other grew until they coalesced into a self-styled movement. They included William Gibson, Bruce Sterling, Rudy Rucker, John Shirley, and Lewis Shiner. As their stories hit home, their ideas about science fiction began to gain traction, in part due to the withering attacks on the status quo that appeared in their fanzine-cum-propaganda organ, *Cheap Truth*. Published pseudonymously by Bruce Sterling, not only did it slag SF's literary establishment, which produced "stories that lie gasping and wall-eyed with anemia," but it also ridiculed those up-and-coming writers who had yet to acknowledge the cyberpunk agenda. "SF must stop recycling the same half-baked traditions about the nature of the human future. And its most formally gifted authors must escape their servant's mentality and learn to stop aping their former masters in the literary mainstream. Until that happens, SF will continue sliding through obsolescence toward outright necrophilia" (Sterling, 1983, 1).

Couched in such hyperbole, the cyberpunks' message was greeted with bemusement or outright hostility by many working in the genre. For each of those who came to share the cyberpunk sensibility, writers like Mark Laidlaw, Tom Maddox, and most notably Pat Cadigan, there seemed to be three naysayers ready to decry it as a sham or a clever public relations ploy. In the otherwise celebratory *Cyberpunk* issue of the *Mississippi Review*, several irate critics fired back. "What we have here, folks," argued Gregory Benford, "is a marketing strategy masquerading as a literary movement" (McCaffery, 1988, 24). David Brin agreed: "Nitty gritty time? "Cyberpunk" is nothing more or less than the best publicity gimmick to come to Speculative/Fiction in years. Adherents make their grand pronouncements and thereby attract roving press flocks, always eager to do a piece on the latest rebel" (26). Fred Pohl dismissed the movement entirely: "I have yet to find a character in any Cyberpunk story that I care about, or indeed believe" (46).

In order to showcase their fiction, Sterling floated a proposal for an anthology of the movement's greatest hits. Editor David Hartwell, who ultimately bought *Mirrorshades: The Cyberpunk Anthology,* remembered some of the negotiation over the book's contents, "As I recall, he had six writers (two of them collaborators of the original four) and I said that there had to be twelve to make a movement, or words to that effect. He said it would be no problem to include twelve, and so he surprised people such as James Patrick Kelly, Greg Bear, and Paul DiFilipo by making them part of the movement and including them in *Mirrorshades*" (Kelly, 2001, 9).

It is with *Mirrorshades,* intended to be the definitive statement of what the first cyberpunks were all about, that the debate over ownership begins. With the publication of this book, it was now officially possible to write like a cyberpunk without being one. After *Mirrorshades* we are no longer necessarily talking about the group of writers called cyberpunks, but rather *cyberpunk*, the literary genre that was soon to become a cultural phenomenon.

Image and Idea

Had its critics been right, there would have been no cyberpunk phenomenon. But as Sterling laid out cyberpunk's central concerns in the introduction to *Mirrorshades*, he was, in fact, describing a different direction for modern science fiction. "Certain central themes spring up repeatedly in cyberpunk. The theme of body invasion: prosthetic limbs, implanted circuitry, cosmetic surgery, genetic alteration. The even more powerful theme of mind invasion: brain-computer interfaces, artificial intelligence, neurochemistry—techniques radically redefining the nature of humanity, the nature of the self" (Sterling, 1986, xi).

The cyberpunks were reacting to the kinds of traditionally technophilic stories in which humanity explores and changes the physical world—far-flung space-based fiction in particular. It did not escape their attention that a decade had passed since the last moon landing with no return in prospect. So they advocated for a change of focus.

Their stories were more personal, using technology to explore what it meant to be human. They wanted science fiction to acknowledge that changes to what we do are not as important as changes to who we are. "For the cyberpunks, by stark contrast, technology is visceral. It is not the bottled genie of remote Big Science boffins; it is pervasive, utterly intimate. Not outside us, but next to us. Under our skin; often inside our minds" (Sterling, 1986, xi). Were the cyberpunks, in fact, the only ones addressing these issues? Of course not. Not only members of their own generation, but many established writers were thinking very hard about the impact of pervasive computing and invasive enhancement. But cyberpunks were reliably obsessive about these matters. And for a time, cyberpunk's flamboyant style and uncompromising attitude were at least as important as the quality of its ideas.

At the outset, the cyberpunks believed they were creating a renegade genre. They were new on the literary scene, at once ambitious to make their mark and dismissive of much of what had come before them. The heroes of their stories were technological outlaws, as alienated from their dystopian worlds as the core cyberpunk writers were from mainstream science fiction. Indeed, it can be instructive to map some of the earliest cyberpunk plots onto the careers of their creators. If the "cyber" in cyberpunk points to the extrapolations of the protogenre, then the "punk" is all about presentation. "Cyberpunk work is marked by its visionary intensity. Its writers prize the bizarre, the surreal, the formerly unthinkable. They are willing—eager, even—to take an idea and unflinchingly push it past its limits" (Sterling, 1986, xii). They do this to achieve "classically punk shock value" according to Sterling, who again and again links the cyberpunk literary style to the music of the time. "With this intensity of vision comes strong imaginative concentration. Cyberpunk is widely known for its telling use of detail, its carefully constructed intricacy, its willingness to carry extrapolation into the fabric of daily life. It features 'crammed' prose: rapid, dizzying bursts of novel information, sensory overload that submerges the reader in the literary equivalent of the hard-rock 'wall of sound'" (xiii).

If there was a flaw in the conceptualization of cyberpunk in this founding text, it is the symbolism of the mirrorshades. According to Sterling, "By hiding the eyes, mirrorshades prevent the forces of normalcy from realizing that one is crazed and possibly dangerous" (Sterling, 1986, ix). Well, maybe. But they are also an affectation tied to a particular time and place. When we revisit near future science fiction, we tend to judge how well it has aged. Quaint is the enemy of cutting edge. Unfortunately, mirrorshades make an eighties fashion statement that also reminds us that much of the tech in early cyberpunk has gone out of date and that some of the extrapolation has proved wrong.

Nowhere is the obsolescence problem more evident than in *Neuromancer*. How could it be otherwise? When William Gibson wrote what many consider to be his masterpiece, there were no mice, no hard disks. In those the pre-Macintosh days, before Windows opened, there were just over one thousand internet hosts; in 2010 we are now approaching a billion. And Gibson famously was never a fan of computers; he wrote the book on a 1927 model portable typewriter. Consider the opening line, once cited as an exemplar of his deft use of language: "The sky above the port was the color of television, tuned to a dead channel" (Gibson, 1984, 3). The image, undeniably vivid to his contemporaries, cries out for a footnote to explain it to twenty-first century readers. What color is a digital TV screen tuned to no channel?

And yet *Neuromancer* is without doubt the first and most important cyberpunk novel. It is lightning fast and always surprising. It manages to capture all the colors of alienation in an array of characters that shimmer on the page. Yes, it's a tour of outlaw neighborhoods filled with people you would hate to meet in a dark alley, but that's what Gibson was aiming for and he hit the mark exactly. Not surprisingly, it manages to touch on almost all of the themes in the cyberpunk agenda as outlined in *Mirrorshades*. And although it is sometimes prone to rhetorical excess, it is nonetheless one of the most stylish novels ever written in the speculative genre. As a model for those who would come after, its "crammed" prose suggests a society that not only its characters truly inhabit, but that also demands to see the reader's passport. You don't just visit Gibson's Sprawl and leave; you get it all over you and it won't come off. Consider:

> The Panther Modern leader, who introduced himself as Lupus Yonderboy, wore a polycarbon suit with a recording feature that allowed him to replay backgrounds at will. Perched on the edge of Case's worktable like some kind of state of the art gargoyle, he regarded Case and Armitage with hooded eyes. He smiled. His hair was pink. A rainbow forest of microsofts bristled behind his left ear; the ear was pointed, tufted with more pink hair. (Gibson, 1984, 67)

Take that, Isaac Asimov!

Not Dead Yet

By 1986, cyberpunk was ascendant. *Neuromancer* had won the Nebula, the Hugo, and Philip K. Dick Award. *Mirrorshades* had been published, making both an artistic and ideological case for the new genre. Still it came as something of a surprise when the last *Cheap Truth* came out. In it, Sterling issued a cryptic farewell, "I hereby declare the revolution over. Long live the provisional government" (Sterling, 1986, 2). While this was, in retrospect, a shrewd move, it caused some confusion at the time. Was cyberpunk also over? It seemed possible, as some of the first cyberpunks were finding the label a mixed blessing. And without the party organ to enforce ideological purity, how would anyone know what was cyberpunk and what wasn't? Sterling had drawn the cyberpunk struggle to a close. What was next?

Who Owned Cyberpunk?

But even though *Cheap Truth* seemed to be declaring that the party was over, writers of talent and ambition still wanted to celebrate cyberpunk values. Novels proliferated, many in series. Of the first cyberpunks, William Gibson returned to the Sprawl in *Count Zero* (1986) and *Mona Lisa Overdrive* (1988). John Shirley began his A Song Called Youth series with *Eclipse* (1985). Rudy Rucker followed up 1982's *Software* with *Wetware* (1988), putting his own unique spin on cyberpunk. Both of these novels won the Philip K. Dick Award. Lewis Shiner published just one cyberpunk novel, *Frontera* (1984) before distancing himself from the "c-word," as some veterans of the movement were calling it, with *Deserted Cities of the Heart* (1988). With *Schismatrix* (1985) Bruce Sterling launched cyberpunk into space. Set in the twenty-third century, it described a posthuman society bifurcated into Shapers, who altered themselves biologically and Mechanists, who used cybernetic and prosthetic enhancements. His next novel, *Islands in the Net* (1988) might be described as cyberpunk 2.0. It depicted a world similar to those commonly associated with cyberpunk, but his story was told from the point of view of a stakeholder in the world. Its protagonist was a *mom*; she was part of a stable nuclear family and worked in public relations for a global corporation.

It was not only the original five who were busy. While some of the writers in *Mirrorshades* turned away from the work or fell silent, others prospered. Pat Cadigan published novels *Mindplayers* (1987) and *Synners* (1991), contemplating the future of the mind with a welcome dash of dark humor too often missing from her male colleagues. Greg Bear, whose work shared DNA with cyberpunk but was definitely of a different species, expanded his award-winning story "Blood Music" into a 1985 novel of the same name. But the prolific Bear was also busy publishing novels of alien contact, global catastrophe, and elves. Meanwhile, three writers who might well have been in the sequel to *Mirrorshades* had there been one, Walter Jon Williams, George Alec Effinger, and Richard Kadrey, published *Hardwired* (1986), *When Gravity Fails* (1986), and *Metrophage* (1988), respectively. And these were just some of the best novels; there was an equal amount of fine short fiction.

While this flood of pharmaceutical-grade cyberpunk during the mid-to-late eighties marked what could be considered its Golden Age, plenty of shallow imitations and derivative works appeared as well. Some writers and readers got caught up in the cyberpunk fashion statement; others naively identified with the antiheroes fighting soulless corporations as they prowled the mean streets of the future. While the ideas behind cyberpunk became even more relevant as internet culture spread and biotech advanced, the genre's neo-noir furniture began to seem worn and a just a bit dowdy.

The Street also Runs Uptown

However, a funny thing happened as cyberpunk threatened to slide into cliché. In Gibson's 1982 story "Burning Chrome" there was a line that the cyberpunks were fond of quoting: "the street finds its own uses for things" (Gibson, 2003, 199). They meant to say that we will repurpose technology—or anything, for that matter—for whatever suits us without regard for the designer's intentions. In the context of the Gibson story, the "street" refers to the shadowy hacker subculture. But all kinds of people live on the metaphorical street, including suburban teens, ad executives, civil libertarians, software engineers and movie producers. And many of them took a sudden interest in this once obscure corner of science fiction. Before anyone realized what was happening, liquid sense of wonder had sloshed out of its genre containment and spilled across popular culture. Cyberpunk was hip, even glamorous. William Gibson in *Rolling Stone*! Does a cameo in a television miniseries—about cyberpunk! His neologism, "cyberspace," is enshrined in the *Oxford English Dictionary*! Bruce Sterling gets the cover of the debut issue of *Wired*! But although cyberpunk made some of its practitioners into stars, the excitement was really all about the new genre.

And what exactly caught people's fancy? Perhaps it was that cyberpunk was a kind of science fiction ordinary folks might actually live. Nobody in her right mind expected to crew on the *Starship Enterprise* or jaunt back to the Jurassic, but for a thousand dollars or so you could stick your head through the screen of a personal computer and breathe 100 percent pure cyberspace.

Movies quoted the familiar tropes. Actually the first and best cyberpunk movie was *Blade Runner* (1982). In retrospect, perhaps it marks the real beginning of cyberpunk, since the first cyberpunks were largely unknown short story writers when it was released. But the film received mixed reviews and did poorly at the box office; only later did it become a cult favorite. Meanwhile *Robocop* (1987), *Akira* (1988), *Twelve Monkeys* (1995), *Strange Days* (1995), *Ghost in the Shell* (1995), *Gattaca* (1997), *Dark City* (1998), *The Matrix* (1999), *The Thirteenth*

Floor (1999), and *Minority Report* (2002) were all demonstrably under the influence. And these were just the films that bear close scrutiny; dozens of other knockoffs ranged from tolerable to unwatchable. Cyberpunk fared less well on television, with *Max Headroom* (1987–88) being the only notable example. *Wild Palms* (1993), the largely forgotten miniseries in which Gibson appeared, was a hodgepodge.

The Japanese were particularly avid producers and consumers; manga versions of *Ghost in the Shell* (1989) and *Akira* (1982–90) preceded their anime adaptations. Other notable manga include *Battle Angel Alita* (1990), *BLAME!* (1998–2003) and *Gantz* (2000). Meanwhile, after an abortive attempt to adapt *Neuromancer* (1989) into a graphic novel, English-language cyberpunk comics flourished with *The Hacker Files* (1992–93) written by first cyberpunk Lewis Shiner, *Ghost Rider 2099* (1994–96), *Transmetropolitan* (1997–2002) and *Singularity 7* (2004) being notable examples. The gaming industry too embraced cyberpunk. In 1988 *Neuromancer* was loosely adapted into a computer adventure game. It was followed by hits like *Beneath A Steel Sky* (1994), *BioForge* (1995), *System Shock 2* (1999), and *Deus Ex* (2000). There were also board games and role-playing games, the best known of which was the *Cyberpunk* series, beginning in 1988. In 1990 the Secret Service raided the headquarters of Steve Jackson Games, ostensibly because information in the *Cyberpunk* sourcebook it published could be used to commit computer crime. Although this proved not to be the case, the incident quickly became a cause célèbre and helped motivate computer savvy civil libertarians to form the Electronic Freedom Foundation. Even some rock albums displayed distinct influences; among them were Sigue Sigue Sputnik's *Flaunt It* (1986), Warren Zevon's *Transverse City* (1989), Billy Idol's *Cyberpunk* (1993), and David Bowie's *Outside* (1995).

What many of these works captured was more the style than the substance of cyberpunk. That was to be expected. More troubling to those who took the form seriously were those commercial interests which used cyberpunk as a brand name for items and services that had little or nothing to do with the new genre. CyberPunk Software offered Virtual Woman 2000, a computerized stripper program with a crude AI which could parse pickup lines. Vendors sold all kinds of cyberpunk jewelry; you could own a Cyberpunk TS100 stainless steel watch for about a hundred dollars. There were trademark applications for Cyberbroker, Cyberjunk, Cyberspace Holding Company, and Cyberswain. Happily, an attempt to found the Cyberpunk CPU University School for the Digitally Enabled never got off the ground.

Not only did the cyberpunks no longer own cyberpunk, but print science fiction seemed to have lost its claim as well.

Post It

Even as cyberpunk was hacking a niche into popular culture, some key players in science fiction were busy burying it. In the opinion of *The Encyclopedia of Science Fiction*, "If cyberpunk is dead in the 1990s—as several critics have claimed—it is as a result of euthanasia from within the family" (Nicholls, 1993, 290). This was due in part to the commodification of the bling, but there was also telling criticism from within the genre. It had always been an embarrassment that so few women wrote it, but feminist critics pointed out that while cyberpunk claimed to be revolutionary, it was still dominated by heteronormative conventions of gender, sexuality and power. The plots often expressed male anxiety over all those intimate enhancements to the body, there was a huge disparity between the number of strong male characters and the number of strong female characters and gay and lesbian characters were all but invisible. In short, the movement had inherited some of the conservative social values of the mainstream science fiction it sought to reform.

Moreover, the classic cyberpunk protagonists, alienated and emotionally crippled outsiders, had grown as tiresome as the classic cyberpunk worlds they lived in. The creators of the website CybRpunk actually outlined a formula for wannabe cyberpunks. All the familiar components were assembled for the Do-It-Yourself crowd. The subcultures: "Drug Culture is going to figure big"; the settings: "The USA is broken up into city-states, ruled by corporate dictators"; the hardware: "Personal tanks will be popular"; and the wetware: "Neural jacks are possible, but difficult" (Wronkiewicz and Motley, 1996). As time passed, not only did the traditional trappings become clichéd, but technological and social developments made them seem bad extrapolation.

In 1998, writer and critic Lawrence Person published "Notes Toward a Postcyberpunk Manifesto." It begins:

> Bud, from Neal Stephenson's *The Diamond Age*, is a classic cyberpunk protagonist. An aggressive, black-leather clad criminal loner with cybernetic body augmentations (including a neurolinked skull gun), Bud makes his living first as a drug runner's decoy, then by terrorizing tourists for money.
>
> All of which goes a long way toward explaining why his ass gets wasted on page 37 of a 455 page novel.
>
> Welcome to the postcyberpunk era. (Person, 1998)

With the publication of *Snow Crash* (1992) and Hugo Award winning *The Diamond Age* (1995) Neal Stephenson established as good a claim as any to be called the first postcyberpunk. The genre had been mutating, as can be seen from novels like Pat Cadigan's *Fools*

(1992), Melissa Scott's *Trouble and Her Friends* (1994) and *Night Sky Mine* (1997), and Paul J. McAuley's *Fairyland* (1995). Both *Fools* and *Fairyland* won the Arthur C. Clarke Award. Greg Egan's extraordinary hard science novels *Quarantine* (1992) and the Campbell Award winning *Permutation City* (1994), clearly shared themes with cyberpunk. Meanwhile *Mirrorshades* veteran Paul Di Filippo offered up *Ribofunk* (1996), a collection of contrarian biological riffs on Cyberpunk. Bruce Sterling with *Heavy Weather* (1994) and *Holy Fire* (1996) and William Gibson with his Bridge trilogy *Virtual Light* (1993), *Idoru* (1996), and *All Tomorrow's Parties* (1999) were also redefining the genre.

Reviewers and critics had no problem identifying cyberpunk themes and techniques in these works. For example, the take-no-prisoners "crammed" style, heavily laden with neologisms, had not gone away:

Pooning a bimbo box takes more skill than a ped would ever imagine, because of their very roadunworthiness, their congenital lack of steel or other ferrous matter for the MagnaPoon to bite down on. Now they have superconducting poons that stick to aluminum body work by inducing eddy currents in the actual flesh of the car, turning it into an unwilling electromagnet, but Y. T. does not have one of these. They are the trademark of the hardcore Burbclave surfer, which, despite this evening's entertainment, she is not. Her poon will only stick to steel, iron, or (slightly) to nickel. The only steel in a bimbo box of this make is in the frame. (Stephenson 1992, 29)

These postcyberpunk books were still passionately engaged with bleeding edge technologies in information-saturated worlds. The internet had helped writers give cyberspace a needed makeover. It had become as much a utility as heat or electricity—accessible, if not to everyone, then to a significantly larger and thus more diverse population. Cyberspace now encompassed virtual worlds and augmented sensoria; coping with mediated reality remained a necessary life skill. The Human Operating System was still subject to revision; add-ons continued to be commonplace. Advances in genomics and bioengineering had made the cyberpunk's visionary redesign of nature in general and the human body in particular seem plausible, if not inevitable. The stories were still set mostly on earth—space travel, if it occurred at all, was an afterthought.

But if these books were indeed postcyberpunk, then how were they different from its original incarnation? Unfortunately, it is impossible to cite a specific date and consign all works written before it to cyberpunk and all written after to postcyberpunk. Some differ in style but not so much in content, others explore the conceptual boundaries of the genre.

While characters in a postcyberpunk novel may be alienated from their society, they are usually integrated into it. They often have jobs and families; they value membership in a community. The cowboys and outlaws of cyberpunk stood outside their societies. Because their perspectives on their worlds were skewed, our understanding of them was imperfect. Who was designing and building and maintaining all the advanced computers in a traditional cyberpunk story? Cyberspace needs electricians! And while postcyberpunk worlds may be grim, they are usually not true dystopias. Or rather, they are no more dystopic than the world that presents itself to us in today's dreary headlines. Postcyberpunk writing can be playful. With the revolutionary fervor of the early eighties no longer necessary, there is more room in the genre for irony and humor. Of course, these writers are keenly aware that the technologies they invoke raise the possibility of a post-human future. And while the advent of Vernor Vinge's Singularity is by no means certain, it can't be entirely discounted.

In the first decade of the new century, postcyberpunk continues to flourish. More women have embraced the genre, for example Justina Robson with *Silver Screen* (1999), *Mappa Mundi* (2001), and *Natural History* (2003); Chris Moriarty with *Spin State* (2003) and *Spin Control* (2006); and Elizabeth Bear with her Jenny Casey trilogy, *Hammered*, *Scardown*, and *Worldwired*, all of which were published in 2005. Fine novels like Will Shetterly's *Chimera* (2000); Richard Morgan's *Altered Carbon* (2002); Ian McDonald's *River of Gods* (2004) and *Cyberabad Days* (2009); Charles Stross's *Accelerando* (2005) and its sequel *Glasshouse* (2006); Cory Doctorow's *Down and Out in the Magic Kingdom* (2003), *Little Brother* (2008), and *Makers* (2009); and Paolo Bacigalupi's *Windup Girl* (2009) have maintained the high standards set by the early cyberpunks. In fact, these writers have been recognized as among the best of their literary generation. *Down and Out in the Magic Kingdom*, *Hammered*, and *Accelerando* all won Locus Awards for Best First Novel. *Altered Carbon* and *Spin Control* were Philip K. Dick Award winners. Justina Robson has twice been shortlisted for British Science Fiction Association Best Novel award and Ian McDonald has won for *River of Gods*. *Little Brother* received the John W. Campbell Memorial Award, and *Windup Girl* was honored with a Hugo, a Nebula, and the Campbell Award.

Cyberpunk Not Only Lives, It Rules!
Or does it? While both cyberpunk and postcyberpunk still have currency among critics, the distinction between them continues to blur.

The eighties are history, and the movement has moved on. The literary sins of cyberpunk have been forgiven, or at least nobody commits them anymore. Unlike their predecessors, the postcyberpunk as a group lack cohesion of purpose. Because they live and write in a culture that the cyberpunks helped to create, we can point to certain of their techniques or habits of thought and say *See there? That's Cyberpunk*! But more and more often the terms *cyberpunk* and *postcyberpunk* describe tropes, and not intentions. The ideas that genre writers grapple with in the twenty-first century are no longer tied to any specific ideology. They are now the provenance of science fiction.

Which means the revolution is truly over.

Owning up

In the interest of full disclosure, I should reveal my bias in these matters. I have been at once an observer and a sometime participant in the evolution of this genre. I had a story in *Mirrorshades*. I have written many other stories which, if not cyberpunk, then are in close dialogue with it, including a novel published in 1994. In 2007 John Kessel and I edited *Rewired: The Post-Cyberpunk Anthology*, which surveyed the impact of cyberpunk in the period from 1996 to the present—well after its Golden Age. The opinions expressed in that book are repeated above. Some are controversial; writers even more closely associated with the movement and its aftermath than I saw things differently.

Like any critic who takes on the dubious task of canon building, I have here claimed a kind of ownership of the genre by listing those who I think belong and omitting those who I believe do not. If I have overlooked your favorite writer, I apologize. However, that is why I strongly caution you to remember this:

I don't own cyberpunk. We all do.

Bibliography

Clute, John, and Peter Nicholls. *The Encyclopedia of Science Fiction*. New York: St. Martin's, 1993.

Dozois, Gardner. *The Year's Best Science Fiction, Second Annual Collection*. New York: Bluejay Books, 1985.

Gibson, William. *Burning Chrome*. New York: Eos, 2003.

———. *Neuromancer*. New York: Ace, 1984.

Kelly, James Patrick. "On the Net: Cyberpunk." *Asimov's Science Fiction*, January 2001.

McCaffery, Larry, ed. *Mississippi Review* 16, no. 2/3 (1988): 16–65.

Person, Lawrence. "Notes Toward a Postcyberpunk Manifesto." *Nova Express* 4, no. 4 (1998).

Stephenson, Neal. *Snow Crash*. New York: Bantam Spectra, 1992.

Sterling, Bruce. *Cheap Truth 2*. http://www.joelbenford.plus.com/sterling/ct/ct02.txt.

———. *Mirrorshades: The Cyberpunk Anthology*. New York, Arbor House, 1986.

———. *The Last Cheap Truth*. http://www.joelbenford.plus.com/sterling/ct/ctlast.txt.

Wronkiewicz, Ken, and Marshall Motley. *CybRpunk*. http://gearheads.wirewd.com/cybrpunk. Accessed May 13, 2013.

Recommended Reading

Cadigan, Pat, ed. *The Ultimate Cyberpunk*. New York: I Books, 2004.

Gibson, William. *Neuromancer*. New York: Ace, 1984.

Kelly, James Patrick, and John Kessel, eds. *Rewired: The Post Cyberpunk Anthology*. San Francisco: Tachyon Publications, 2007.

McCaffery, Larry, ed. *Storming the Reality Studio: A Casebook of Cyberpunk & Postmodern Science Fiction*. Durham, NC: Duke University Press, 1992.

Stephenson, Neal. *The Diamond Age; or, a Young Lady's Illustrated Primer*. New York: Bantam Spectra, 1995.

Sterling, Bruce. *Mirrorshades: The Cyberpunk Anthology*. New York: Arbor House, 1986.

Stross, Charles. *Accelerando*. New York: Ace, 2006.

The Best Christmas Ever

AUNTIE EM'S MAN WAS not doing well at all. He had been droopy and gray ever since the neighbor Mr. Kimura had died, shuffling around the house in nothing but socks and bathrobe. He had even lost interest in the model train layout that he and the neighbor were building in the garage. Sometimes he stayed in bed until eleven in the morning and had ancient Twinkies for lunch. He had a sour, vinegary smell. By midafternoon he'd be asking her to mix strange ethanol concoctions like Brave Little Toasters and Tin Honeymoons. After he had drunk five or six, he would stagger around the house mumbling about the big fires he'd fought with Ladder Company No. 3 or the wife he had lost in the Boston plague. Sometimes he would just cry.

Begin Interaction 4022932

"Do you want to watch *Annie Hall*?" Auntie Em asked.

The man perched on the edge of the Tyvola sofa in the living room, elbows propped on knees, head sunk into hands.

"*The General*? *Monty Python and the Holy Grail*? *Spaced Out*?"

"I hate that robot." He tugged at his thinning hair and snarled. "I hate robots."

Auntie Em did not take this personally—she was a biop, not a robot. "I could call Lola. She's been asking after you."

"I'll bet." Still, he looked up from damp hands. "I'd rather have Kathy."

This was a bad sign. Kathy was the lost wife. The girlfriend biop could certainly assume that body; she could look like anyone the man wanted. But while the girlfriend biop could pretend, she could never be the wife that the man missed. His reactions to the Kathy body were always erratic and sometimes dangerous.

"I'll nose around town," said Auntie Em. "I heard Kathy was off on a business trip, but maybe she's back."

"Nose around," he said and then reached for the glass on the original Noguchi coffee table with spread fingers, as if he thought it might try to leap from his grasp. "You do that." He captured it on the second attempt.

End Interaction 4022932

#

The man was fifty-six years old and in good health, considering. His name was Albert Paul Hopkins but none of the biops called him that. Auntie Em called him Bertie. The girlfriend called him sweetie or Al. The pal biops called him Al or Hoppy or Sport. The stranger biops called him Mr. Hopkins or sir. The animal biops didn't speak much, but the dog called him Buddy and the cat called him Mario.

When Auntie Em beamed a summary of the interaction to the girlfriend biop, the girlfriend immediately volunteered to try the Kathy body again. The girlfriend had been desperate of late, since the man didn't want anything to do with her. His slump had been hard on her, hard on Auntie Em too. Taking care of the man had changed the biops. They were all so much more emotional than they had been when they were first budded.

But Auntie Em told the girlfriend to hold off. Instead she decided to throw a Christmas. She hadn't done Christmas in almost eight months. She'd given him a *Gone with the Wind* Halloween and a Fourth of July with whistling busters, panoramas, phantom balls and double-break shells, but those were only stopgaps. The man needed cookies, he needed presents, he was absolutely aching for a sleigh filled with Christmas cheer. So she beamed an alert to all of her biops and assigned roles. She warned them that if this wasn't the best Christmas ever, they might lose the last man on earth.

#

Auntie Em spent three days baking cookies. She dumped eight sticks of fatty acid triglycerides, four cups of $C_{12}H_{22}O_{11}$, four vat-grown ova, four teaspoons of flavor potentiator, twelve cups of milled grain endosperm and five teaspoons each of $NaHCO_3$ and $KHC_4H_4O_6$ into the bathtub and then trod on the mixture with her best baking boots. She rolled the dough and then pulled cookie cutters off the top shelf of the pantry: the mitten and the dollar sign and the snake and the double-bladed ax. She dusted the cookies with red nutriceutical sprinkles, baked them at $190^\circ C$, and brought a plate to the man while they were still warm.

The poor thing was melting into the recliner in the television room. He clutched a half-full tumbler of Sins-of-the-Mother, as if it were the anchor that was keeping him from floating out of the window. He had done nothing but watch classic commercials with the sound off since he had fallen out of bed. The cat was curled on the man's lap, pretending to be asleep.

Begin Interaction 4022947

"Cookies, Bertie," said Auntie Em. "Fresh from the oven, oven fresh." She set the plate down on the end table next to the Waterford lead crystal vase filled with silk daffodils.

"Not hungry," he said. On the mint-condition 34-inch Sony Hi-Scan television Ronald McDonald was dancing with some kids.

Auntie Em stepped in front of the screen, blocking his view. "Have you decided what you want for Christmas, dear?"

"It isn't Christmas." He waved her away from the set but she didn't budge. He did succeed in disturbing the cat, which stood, arched its back and then dropped to the floor.

"No, of course it isn't." She laughed. "Christmas isn't until next week."

He aimed the remote at the set and turned up the sound. A man was talking very fast. "Two all-beef patties, special sauce, lettuce, cheese . . ."

Auntie Em pressed the off button with her knee. "I'm talking to you, Bertie."

The man lowered the remote. "What's today?"

"Today is Friday." She considered. "Yes, Friday."

"No, I mean the date."

"The date is . . . let me see. The twenty-first."

His skin temperature had risen from 33°C to 37°. "The twenty-first of what?" he said.

She stepped away from the screen. "Have another cookie, Bertie."

"All right." He turned the television on and muted it. "You win." A morose Maytag repairman slouched at his desk, waiting for the phone to ring. "I know what I want," said the man. "I want a Glock 17."

"And what is that, dear?"

"It's a nine millimeter handgun."

"A handgun, oh my." Auntie Em was so flustered that she ate one of her own cookies, even though she had extinguished her digestive track for the day. "For shooting? What would you shoot?"

"I don't know." He broke the head off a gingerbread man. "A reindeer. The TV. Maybe one of you."

"Us? Oh, Bertie—one of us?"

He made a gun out of his thumb and forefinger and aimed. "Maybe just the cat." His thumb came down.

The cat twitched. "Mario," it said and nudged the man's bare foot with its head. "No, Mario."

On the screen the Jolly Green Giant rained peas down on capering elves.

End Interaction 4022947

#

Begin Interaction 4023013

The man stepped onto the front porch of his house and squinted at the sky, blinking. It was late spring and the daffodils were nodding in a warm breeze. Auntie Em pulled the sleigh to the bottom of the steps and honked the horn. It played the first three notes of "Jingle Bells." The man turned to go back into the house but the girlfriend biop took him by the arm. "Come on now, sweetie," she said and steered him toward the steps.

The girlfriend had assumed the Donna Reed body the day before, but unlike previous Christmases, the man had taken no sexual interest in her. She was wearing the severe black dress with the white lace collar from the last scene of *It's a Wonderful Life*. The girlfriend looked as worried about the man as Mary had been about despairing George Bailey. All the biops were worried, thought Auntie Em. They would be just devastated if anything happened to him. She waved gaily and hit the horn again. *Beep-beep-BEEP!*

The dog and the cat had transformed themselves into reindeer for the outing. The cat got the red nose. Three of the animal biops had assumed reindeer bodies too. They were all harnessed to the sleigh, which hovered about a foot off the ground. As the man stumped down the steps, Auntie Em discouraged the antigrav and the runners crunched against gravel. The girlfriend bundled the man aboard.

"Do you see who we have guiding the way?" said Auntie Em. She beamed the cat and it lit up its nose. "See?"

"Is that the fake cop?" The man coughed. "Or the fake pizza guy? I can't keep them straight."

"On Dasher, now Dancer, now Comet and Nixon," cried Auntie Em as she encouraged the antigrav. "To the mall, Rudolf, and don't bother to slow down for yellow lights!" She cracked the whip and away they went, down the driveway and out into the world.

The man lived at the edge of the biop compound, away from the bustle of the spaceport and the accumulatorium with its bulging galleries of authentic human artifacts and the vat where new biops were budded off the master template. They drove along the perimeter road. The biops were letting the forest take over here, and saplings of birch and hemlock sprouted from the ruins of the town.

The sleigh floated across a bridge and Auntie Em started to sing. "Over the river and through the woods . . ." but when she glanced over her shoulder and saw the look on the man's face, she stopped. "Is something wrong, Bertie dear?"

"Where are you taking me?" he said. "I don't recognize this road."

"It's a secret," said Auntie Em. "A Christmas secret."

His blood pressure had dropped to 93/60. "Have I been there before?"

"I wouldn't think so. No."

The girlfriend clutched the man's shoulder. "Look," she said. "Sheep."

Four ewes had gathered at the river's edge to drink, their stumpy tails twitching. They were big animals; their long, tawny fleeces made them look like walking couches. A brown man on a dromedary camel watched over them. He was wearing a satin robe in royal purple with gold trim at the neck. When Auntie Em beamed him the signal, he tapped the line attached to the camel's nose peg and the animal turned to face the road.

"One of the wise men," said Auntie Em.

"The king of the shepherds," said the girlfriend.

As the sleigh drove by, the wise man tipped his crown to them. The sheep looked up from the river and bleated, "Happy holidays."

"They're so cute," said the girlfriend. "I wish we had sheep."

The man sighed. "I could use a drink."

"Not just yet, Bertie," said Auntie Em. "But I bet Mary packed your candy."

The girlfriend pulled a plastic pumpkin from underneath the seat. It was filled with leftovers from the Easter they'd had last month. She held it out to the man and shook it. It was filled with peeps and candy corn and squirtgum and chocolate crosses. He pulled a peep from the pumpkin and sniffed it suspiciously.

"It's safe, sweetie," said the girlfriend. "I irradiated everything just before we left."

There were no cars parked in the crumbling lot of the Walmart. They pulled up to the entrance where a Salvation Army Santa stood over a black plastic pot holding a bell. The man didn't move.

"We're here, Al." The girlfriend nudged him. "Let's go."

"What is this?" said the man.

"Christmas shopping," said Auntie Em. "Time to shop."

"Who the hell am I supposed to shop for?"

"Whoever you want," said Auntie Em. "You could shop for us. You could shop for yourself. You could shop for Kathy."

"Auntie Em!" said the girlfriend.

"No," said the man. "Not Kathy."

"Then how about Mrs. Marelli?"

The man froze. "Is that what this is about?"

"It's about Christmas, Al," said the girlfriend. "It's about getting out of the goddamned sleigh and going into the store." She climbed over him and jumped down to the pavement before Auntie Em could discourage the antigrav. She stalked by the Santa and through the entrance without looking back. Auntie Em beamed her a request to come back but she went dark.

"All right," said the man. "You win."

The Santa rang his bell at them as they approached. The man stopped and grasped Auntie Em's arm. "Just a minute," he said and ran back to the sleigh to fetch the plastic pumpkin. He emptied the candy into the Santa's pot.

"God bless you, young man." The Santa knelt and sifted the candy through his red suede gloves as if it were gold.

"Yeah," said the man. "Merry Christmas."

Auntie Em twinkled at the two of them. She thought the man might finally be getting into the spirit of the season.

The store was full of biops, transformed into shoppers. They had stocked the shelves with artifacts authenticated by the accumulatorium: Barbies and Sonys and Goodyears and Dockers; patio furniture and towels and microwave ovens and watches. At the front of the store was an array of polyvinyl chloride spruce trees pre-decorated with bubble lights and topped with glass penguins. Some of the merchandise was new, some used, some broken. The man paid attention to none of it, not even the array of genuine Lionel "O" Scale locomotives and freight cars Auntie Em had ordered specially for this interaction. He passed methodically down the aisles, eyes bright, searching. He strode right by the girlfriend, who was sulking in Cosmetics.

Auntie Em paused to touch her shoulder and beam an encouragement but the girlfriend shook her off. Auntie Em thought she would have to do something about the girlfriend, but she didn't know what exactly. If she sent her back to the vat and replaced her with a new biop, the man would surely notice. The girlfriend and the man had been quite close before the man had slipped into his funk. She knew things about him that even Auntie Em didn't know.

The man found Mrs. Marelli sitting on the floor in the hardware section. She was opening packages of GE Soft White 100-watt light bulbs and then smashing them with a Stanley Workmaster claw hammer. The biop shoppers paid no attention. Only the lead biop of her team, Dr. Watson, seemed to worry about her. He waited with a broom and whenever she tore into a new box of light bulbs, he swept the shards of glass away.

Auntie Em was shocked at the waste. How many pre-extinction light bulbs were left on this world? Twenty thousand? Ten? She wanted to beam a rebuke to Dr. Watson, but she knew he was doing a difficult job as best he could.

"Hello, Ellen." The man knelt next to the woman. "How are you doing?"

She glanced at him, hammer raised. "Dad?" She blinked. "Is that you, Dad?"

"No, it's Albert Hopkins. Al—you know, your neighbor. We've met before. These . . . people introduced us. Remember the picnic? The trip to the spaceport?"

"Picnic?" She shook her head as if to clear it. Ellen Theresa Marelli was eleven years older than the man. She was wearing Bruno Magli black leather flats and a crinkly light blue Land's End dress with a pattern of small dark blue and white flowers. Her hair was gray and a little thin but was nicely cut and permed into tight curls. She was much better groomed than the man, but that was because she couldn't take care of herself anymore and so her biops did everything for her. "I like picnics."

"What are you doing here, Ellen?"

She stared at the hammer as if she were surprised to see it. "Practicing."

"Practicing for what?" He held out his hand for the hammer and she gave it to him.

"Just practicing." She gave him a sly look. "What are *you* doing here?"

"I was hoping to do a little Christmas shopping."

"Oh, is it Christmas?" Her eyes went wide.

"In a couple of days," said the man. "Do you want to tag along?"

She turned to Dr. Watson. "Can I?"

"By all means." Dr. Watson swept the space in front of her.

"Oh goody!" She clapped her hands. "This is just the best." She tried to get up but couldn't until the man and Dr. Watson helped her to her feet. "We'll need a shopping cart," she said.

She tottered to the fashion aisles and tried on sweaters. The man helped her pick out a Ralph Lauren blue cable cardigan that matched her dress. In the housewares section, she decided that she needed a Zyliss garlic press. She spent the most time in the toy aisle, lingering at the Barbies. She didn't care much for the late models, still in their packaging. Instead she made straight for the vintage Barbies and Kens and Francies and Skippers posed around the Barbie Dream House and the Barbie Motor Home. Dr. Watson watched her nervously.

"Look, they even have talking Barbies," she said, picking up a doll in an orange flowered dress. "I had one just like this. With all the blonde hair and everything. See the little necklace? You press the button and . . ."

But the Barbie didn't speak. The woman's mouth set in a grim line and she smashed it against the shelf.

"Ellie," said Dr. Watson. "I wish you wouldn't . . ."

The woman threw the doll at him and picked up another. This was a brunette that was wearing only the top of her hot pink bathing suit. The woman jabbed at the button.

"It's time to get ready for my date with Ken," said the doll in a raspy voice.

"That's better," said the woman.

She pressed the button again and the doll said, "Let's invite the gang over!"

The woman turned to the man and the two biops, clearly excited. "Here." She thrust the doll at Auntie Em, who was nearest to her. "You try." Auntie Em pressed the button.

"I can't wait to meet my friends," said the doll.

"What a lovely toy!" Auntie Em smiled. "She certainly has the Christmas spirit, don't you think, Bertie?"

The man frowned and Auntie Em could tell from the slump of his shoulders that his good mood was slipping away. His heart rate jumped and his eyes were distant, a little misty. The woman must have noticed the change too, because she pointed a finger at Auntie Em.

"You," she said. "You ruin everything."

"Now Mrs. Marelli," she said, "I . . ."

"You're following us." The woman snatched the Barbie away from her. "Who are you?"

"You know me, Mrs. Marelli. I'm Auntie Em."

"That's crazy." The woman's laugh was like a growl. "I'm not crazy."

Dr. Watson beamed a general warning that he was terminating the interaction; seeing the man always upset the woman. "That's enough, Ellen." He grasped her forearm and Auntie Em was relieved to see him paint relaxant onto her skin with his med finger. "I think it's time to go."

The woman shivered. "Wait," she said. "He said it was Christmas." She pointed at the man. "Daddy said."

"We'll talk about that when we get home, Ellen."

"*Daddy*." She shook herself free and flung herself at the man.

The man shook his head. "This isn't . . ."

"*Ssh*. It's okay." The woman hugged him. "Just pretend. That's all we can do, isn't it?" Reluctantly, he returned her embrace. "Daddy." She spoke into his chest. "What are you getting me for Christmas?"

"Can't tell," he said. "It's a secret."

"A Barbie?" She giggled and pulled away from him.

"You'll just have to wait."

"I already know that's what it is."

"But you might forget." The man held out his hand and she gave him the doll. "Now close your eyes."

She shut them so tight that Auntie Em could see her *orbicularis oculi* muscles tremble.

The man touched her forehead. "Daddy says forget." He handed the doll to Dr. Watson, who mouthed *Thank you*. Dr. Watson beamed a request for Auntie Em to hide and she sidled behind the bicycles where the woman couldn't see her. "Okay, Ellen," said the man. "Daddy says open your eyes."

She blinked at him. Daddy," she said softly, "when are you coming home?"

The man was clearly taken aback; there was a beta wave spike in his EEG. "I . . . ah . . ." He scratched the back of his neck. "I don't know," he said. "Our friends here keep me pretty busy."

"I'm so lonely, Daddy." The last woman on earth began to cry.

The man opened his arms to her and they clung to each other, rocking back and forth. "I know," said the man, over and over. "I know."

End Interaction 4023013

\#

Auntie Em, the dog and the cat gathered in the living room of the house, waiting for the man to wake up. She had scheduled the pals, Jeff and Bill, to drop by around noon for sugar cookies and eggnog. The girlfriend was upstairs fuming. She had been Katie Couric, Anna Kournikova and Jacqueline Kennedy since the Walmart trip but the man had never even blinked at her.

The music box was playing "Blue Christmas." The tree was decorated with strings of pinlights and colored packing peanuts. Baseball cards and silver glass balls and plastic army men hung from the branches. Beneath the tree was a modest pile of presents. Auntie Em had picked out one each for the inner circle of biops and signed the man's name to the cards. The rest were gifts for him from them.

Begin Interaction 4023064

"'Morning, Mario," said the cat.

Auntie Em was surprised; it was only eight-thirty. But there was the man propped in the doorway, yawning.

"Merry Christmas, Bertie!" she said.

The dog scrabbled across the room to him. "Buddy, open now, Buddy, open, Buddy, open, open!" It went up on hind legs and pawed his knee.

"Later." The man pushed it away. "What's for breakfast?" he said. "I feel like waffles."

"You want waffles?" said Auntie Em. "Waffles you get."

End Interaction 4023064

She bustled into the kitchen as the man closed the bathroom door behind him. A few minutes later she heard the pipes clang as he turned on the shower. She beamed a revised schedule to the pals, calling for them to arrive within the hour.

Auntie Em could not help but be pleased. This Christmas was already a great success. The man's attitude had changed dramatically after the shopping trip. He was keeping regular hours and drinking much less. He had stopped by the train layout in the garage although all he had done was look at it. Instead he had taken an interest in the garden in the backyard and had spent yesterday weeding the flower beds and digging a new vegetable patch. He had sent the pal Jeff to find seeds he could plant. The biops reported that they had found some peas and corn and string beans—but they were possibly contaminated and might not germinate. She had already warned some of the lesser animal biops that they might have to assume the form of cornstalks and pea vines if the crop failed.

Now if only he would pay attention to the girlfriend.

#

Begin Interaction 4023066

The doorbell gonged the first eight notes of "Silent Night." "Would you get that, Bertie dear?" Auntie Em was pouring freshly budded ova into a pitcher filled with Pet Evaporated Milk.

"It's the pals," the man called from the front hall. "Jeff and . . . I'm sorry, I've forgotten your name."

"Bill."

"Bill, of course. Come in, come in."

A few minutes later, Auntie Em found them sitting on the sofa in the living room. Each of the pals balanced a present on his lap, wrapped in identical green and red paper. They were listening uncomfortably as the cat recited "Twas the Night before Christmas." The man was busy playing Madden NFL 2007 on his Game Boy.

"It's time for sweets and presents, Bertie." Auntie Em set the pitcher of eggnog next to the platter of cookies. She was disturbed that the girlfriend hadn't joined the party yet. She beamed a query but the girlfriend was dark. "Presents and sweets."

The man opened Jeff's present first. It was filled with hand tools for his new garden: a dibbler and a trowel and a claw hoe and a genuine Felco10 Professional Pruner. The dog gave the man a chewable rubber fire hydrant that squeaked when squeezed. The cat gave him an "O" Scale Western Pacific steam locomotive that had belonged to the dead neighbor, Mr. Kimura. The man and the cat exchanged looks briefly and then the cat yawned. The dog nudged his head under all the discarded wrapping paper and the man reached down with the claw hoe and scratched its back. Everyone but the cat laughed.

Next came Bill's present. In keeping with the garden theme of this Christmas, it was a painting of a balding old farmer and a middle-aged woman standing in front of a white house with an odd gothic window. Auntie Em could tell that the man was a farmer because he was holding a pitchfork. The farmer stared out of the painting with a glum intensity; the woman looked at him askance. The curator biop claimed that it was one of the most copied images in the inventory, so Auntie Em was not surprised that the man seemed to recognize it.

"This looks like real paint," he said.

"Yes," said Bill. "Oil on beaverboard."

"What's beaverboard?" said the cat.

"A light, semirigid building material of compressed wood pulp," Bill said. "I looked it up."

The man turned the painting over and brushed his finger across the back. "Where did you get this?" His face was pale.

"From the accumulatorium."

"No, I mean where before then."

Auntie Em eavesdropped as the pal beamed the query. "It was salvaged from the Chicago Art Institute."

"You're giving me the original *American Gothic*?" His voice fell into a hole.

"Is something the matter, Bertie?"

He fell silent for a moment. "No, I suppose not." He shook his head. "It's a very thoughtful gift." He propped the on the mantle, next to his scuffed leather fireman's helmet that the biops had retrieved from the ruins of the Ladder Company No. 3 Firehouse two Christmases ago.

Auntie Em wanted the man to open his big present, but the girlfriend had yet to make her entrance. So instead, she gave the pals their presents from the man. Jeff got the October 1937 issue of *Spicy Adventure Stories*. On the cover a brutish sailor carried a terrified woman in a shredded red dress out of the surf as their ship sank in the background. Auntie Em pretended to be shocked and the man actually chuckled. Bill got a chrome Model 1B14 Toastmaster two-slice toaster. The man took it from him and traced the triple loop logo etched in the side. "My mom had one of these."

Finally there was nothing left to open but the present wrapped in the blue paper with the Santa-in-space print. The man took the Glock 17 out of the box cautiously, as if he were afraid it might go off. It was black with a polymer grip and a four-and-a-half-inch steel barrel. Auntie Em had taken a calculated risk with the pistol. She always tried to give him whatever he asked for, as long as it wasn't too dangerous. He wasn't their captive after all. He was their master.

"Don't worry," she said. "It's not loaded. I looked but couldn't find the right bullets."

"But I did," said the girlfriend, sweeping into the room in the Kathy body. "I looked harder and found hundreds of thousands of bullets."

"Kathy," said Auntie Em, as she beamed a request for her to terminate this unauthorized interaction. "What a nice surprise."

"9mm Parabellum," said the girlfriend. Ten rounds clattered onto the glass top of the Noguchi coffee table. "115 grain. Full metal jacket."

"What are you doing?" said the man.

"You want to shoot someone?" The girlfriend glared at the man and swung her arms wide.

"Kathy," said Auntie Em. "You sound upset, dear. Maybe you should go lie down."

The man returned the girlfriend's stare. "You're not Kathy."

"No," said the girlfriend. "I'm nobody you know."

"Kathy's dead," said the man. "Everybody's dead except for me and poor Ellen Marelli. That's right, isn't it?"

The girlfriend sank to her knees, rested her head on the coffee table, and began to cry. Only biops didn't cry, or at least no biop that Auntie Em had ever heard of. The man glanced around the room for an answer. The pals looked at their shoes and said nothing. "Jingle Bell Rock" tinkled on the music box. Auntie Em felt something swell inside of her and climb her throat until she thought she might burst. If this was what the man felt all the time, it was no wonder he was tempted to drink himself into insensibility.

"Well?" he said.

"Yes," Auntie Em blurted. "Yes, dead, Bertie. All dead."

The man took a deep breath. "Thank you," he said. "Sometimes I can't believe that it really happened. Or else I forget. You make it easy to forget. Maybe you think that's good for me. But I need to know who I am."

"Buddy," said the dog, brushing against him. "Buddy, my Buddy."

The man patted the dog absently. "I could give up. But I won't. I've had a bad spell the last couple of weeks, I know. That's not your fault." He heaved himself off the couch, came around the coffee table, and knelt beside the girlfriend. "I really appreciate that you trust me with this gun. And these bullets too. That's got to be scary, after what I said." The girlfriend watched him scoop up the bullets. "Kathy, I don't need these just now. Would you please keep them for me?"

She nodded.

"Do you know the movie *Miracle on 34th Street*?" He poured the bullets into her cupped hands. "Not the remakes. The first one, with Maureen O'Hara?"

She nodded again.

He leaned close and whispered into her ear. His pulse soared to 93.

She sniffed and then giggled.

"You go ahead," he said to her. "I'll come up in a little while." He gave her a pat on the rear and stood up. The other biops watched him nervously.

"What's with all the long faces?" He tucked the Glock into the waistband of his pants. "You look like them." He waved at the painting of the somber farm folk, whose mood would never, ever change. "It's Christmas Day, people. Let's live it up!"

End Interaction 4023066

#

Over the years, Auntie Em gave the man many more Christmases, not to mention Thanksgivings, Easters, Halloweens, April Fools, and Valentine's Days. But she always said—and no one contradicted her, not the man, not even the girlfriend—that this Christmas was the best ever.

Bibliography

Books

King of the Dogs, Queen of the Cats (novella). Subterranean Press, 2020.

The Promise of Space (collection). Prime Books, 2018.

Mother Go. Audible Audio, 2017.

Masters of Science Fiction: James Patrick Kelly (collection). Centipede Press, 2016.

The Wreck of the Godspeed and Other Stories (collection). Golden Gryphon Press, 2008.

Burn. Tachyon Publications, 2005.

Strange but Not a Stranger (collection). Golden Gryphon Press, 2002.

Think Like a Dinosaur and Other Stories (collection). Golden Gryphon Press, 1997.

Wildlife. Tor Books, 1994.

Heroines (collection). Pulphouse Publishing, 1990.

Look into the Sun. Tor Books, 1989.

Freedom Beach (with John Kessel). Bluejay Books, 1985.

Planet of Whispers. Bluejay Books, 1984.

Anthologies Coedited with John Kessel

Digital Rapture: The Singularity Anthology. Tachyon Publications, 2011.

Kafkaesque: Stories Inspired by Franz Kafka. Tachyon Publications, 2011.

Nebula Awards Showcase. Pyr Books, 2011.

The Secret History of Science Fiction. Tachyon Publications, 2009.

Rewired: The Post-Cyberpunk Anthology. Tachyon Publications, 2007.

Feeling Very Strange: The Slipstream Anthology. Tachyon Publications, 2006.

For a more complete bibliography including short fiction, theatrical plays, and audio plays, visit http://www.jimkelly.net/bibliography.

About the Author

JAMES PATRICK KELLY HAS won the Hugo, Nebula, and Locus awards, and his fiction has been translated into twenty-one languages. He writes a column on the internet for *Asimov's Science Fiction Magazine*. He was a member of the faculty at the Stonecoast Creative Writing MFA Program from 2005 to 2018. Appointed by the governor to the New Hampshire State Council on the Arts, he served for eight years, the last two as chair.

FRIENDS OF PM

These are indisputably momentous times—the financial system is melting down globally and the Empire is stumbling. Now more than ever there is a vital need for radical ideas.

In the years since its founding—and on a mere shoestring—PM Press has risen to the formidable challenge of publishing and distributing knowledge and entertainment for the struggles ahead. With hundreds of releases to date, we have published an impressive and stimulating array of literature, art, music, politics, and culture. Using every available medium, we've succeeded in connecting those hungry for ideas and information to those putting them into practice.

Friends of PM allows you to directly help impact, amplify, and revitalize the discourse and actions of radical writers, filmmakers, and artists. It provides us with a stable foundation from which we can build upon our early successes and provides a much-needed subsidy for the materials that can't necessarily pay their own way. You can help make that happen—and receive every new title automatically delivered to your door once a month—by joining as a Friend of PM Press. And, we'll throw in a free T-shirt when you sign up.

Here are your options:

- **$30 a month**: Get all books and pamphlets plus 50% discount on all webstore purchases
- **$40 a month**: Get all PM Press releases (including CDs and DVDs) plus 50% discount on all webstore purchases
- **$100 a month**: Superstar—Everything plus PM merchandise, free downloads, and 50% discount on all webstore purchases

For those who can't afford $30 or more a month, we have Sustainer Rates at $15, $10, and $5. Sustainers get a free PM Press T-shirt and a 50% discount on all purchases from our website.

Your Visa or Mastercard will be billed once a month, until you tell us to stop. Or until our efforts succeed in bringing the revolution around. Or the financial meltdown of Capital makes plastic redundant. Whichever comes first.

PM Press is an independent, radical publisher of books and media to educate, entertain, and inspire. Founded in 2007 by a small group of people with decades of publishing, media, and organizing experience, PM Press amplifies the voices of radical authors, artists, and activists. Our aim is to deliver bold political ideas and vital stories to all walks of life and arm the dreamers to demand the impossible. We have sold millions of copies of our books, most often one at a time, face to face. We're old enough to know what we're doing and young enough to know what's at stake. Join us to create a better world.

PM Press
PO Box 23912
Oakland, CA 94623
510-658-3906 • info@pmpress.org

PM Press in Europe
europe@pmpress.org
www.pmpress.org.uk